The ace gunner TPF Griffin chop armor-piercing and tracer round mix 25 mm chaingun. Mojo was ready to rock and roll for keeps.

Centering the grounded enemy Super Puma attack helo in his HUD helmet sight visor, he tightened his right hand on the Chain Gun and the left on the grenade launcher triggers. When the glowing red numbers on the digital readout told him he was in range, he laid back hard.

The 25 mm rounds tore into the target at over eight hundred per minute, shattering the spinning turbine compressor blades. The jagged steel blades cut through the pressurized fuel feed lines, spraying JP-4 jet fuel into the air. Hot tracers ignited the volatile fuel, and in seconds, the Puma exploded in a huge ball of flames.

THE DESTROYER
By Warren Murphy and Richard Sapir

Available wherever paperbacks are sold, or order direct from the Publisher. Send cover price plus 50¢ per copy for mailing and handling to Pinnacle Books, Dept. 17-400, 475 Park Avenue South, New York, N.Y. 10016. Residents of New York, New Jersey and Pennsylvania must include sales tax. DO NOT SEND CASH.

CHOPPER COPS

GULF ATTACK

RICK MACKIN

PINNACLE BOOKS
WINDSOR PUBLISHING CORP.

PINNACLE BOOKS

are published by

Windsor Publishing Corp.
475 Park Avenue South
New York, NY 10016

First printing: September, 1990

Printed in the United States of America

Chapter 1

Baja California, Mexico. November 1999

High over the barren coastline of Baja, along the Gulf of California, a pair of sleek dark blue helicopters cut through the crystal clear sky. The bright tropical sun glinted off the yellow letters U.S.T.P.F. painted on the machines' flanks and belly, the initials of the United States Tactical Police Force. Small American flags adorning the choppers' sharply raked, vertical tail fins and large white numbers on their noses were the choppers' only other markings.

Had it not been for the insect eye, tactical sensors on the ships' noses and the 25mm Chain Gun turrets under their bellies, these could have been any police choppers. But, the state-of-the-art sensors and weapons turrets identified these machines as the Bell 506P Griffin helicopters of the TPF's Dragon Flight, the hottest rotary winged aircraft in the skies.

In the right seat of the lead ship, Dragon One Zero, Tactical Police Force Flight Sergeant Rick Wolff flew his machine with precise, delicate adjustments of the controls. Unlike most fixed wing aircraft where the auto-pilot can take over the job of flying while the pilot sits back and relaxes, flying a chopper is a both-hands-on-the-controls job every second that the machine is in the air, but Wolff made it look easy.

But then, it was easy for him. Rick Wolff was the ace flyer in an organization made up of the nation's hottest chopper pilots. His long blond hair and boyish good looks belied the fact that behind his deep green eyes and ready grin was a man who lived only to fly.

Wolff was typical of the men who flew the TPF Griffins.

They were a new breed of police officer, the elite troops of federal law enforcement, the Tactical Police Force. When the Cold War suddenly died in the early 90s, the young men who would have become hot rock military fighter jocks in an earlier era were flying Griffin choppers for the Tac Force's Dragon Flights. As the 21st century approached, these Chopper Cops were America's new "Top Guns" and Rick Wolff was at the head of his class.

As the striking force of the TPF, the Dragon Flights were highly mobile tactical police units that could be deployed anyplace in the country in response to a call. Within hours of a call, four Griffin helicopters, a twenty man Tactical Platoon, a headquarters staff and their support personnel could be on the ground and in the air fighting any crime emergency that was too hot for the local police authorities to handle.

In the rear of the lead Griffin, Wolff's co-pilot and systems operator, Flight Officer Jumal Mugabe, was sprawled across the passenger jump seats trying to get caught up on his sleep. He wore his dark blue flight helmet with the face shield up, but the intercom cord was plugged into the jack. The burly, black gunner couldn't sleep without the soothing, constant chatter of radio traffic in his ears. To shade his eyes, he had laid a gaudy maroon and gold Mexican sombrero across his face. The hat was a souvenir of their visit to the Mexican coastal resort town of Mazatlan where they had attended a convention of Central American police pilots.

Mugabe's sombrero wasn't the only thing the Chopper Cops were bringing back from Mexico. Sitting in Wolff's left seat of the Griffin was a Mexican Federal Police chopper pilot, Lt. Arturo Cuervo. Cuervo was returning to Denver with the chopper cops to go through a transition course in the States to become the first Mexican police pilot qualified to fly the powerful Griffin helicopters.

Police forces all across the nation had been using helicopters for many years, but they had been flying choppers that had originally been designed for civilian use. These machines were expensive to operate and had limited space in their airframes to accommodate the extensive radio and electronic equipment necessary for police work. In the late 1990s, however, a spectacular new machine had been designed to meet the specialized needs of police work, specifically tactical police work, the Bell 506P Griffin.

While the Griffin's lineage went back to the Bell AH-1 Cobra gunships of the Vietnam War, and its systems owed much to the hi-tech military equipment of the mid-'90s, this was the first helicopter that had been built from the ground up strictly for police use.

Designed with low maintenance costs in mind, the Griffin was powered by two small but powerful 750 shaft horsepower General Electric turbines pod mounted externally on the fuselage. Driving a four bladed rigid rotor with a diameter of only 40 feet, the twin turbines could propel the Griffin to speeds of over 250 miles an hour. Both the main rotor and the shrouded tail rotor were designed for noise suppression as well as for maximum maneuverability. Not only was the Griffin quick and stable, it was quiet.

With a flight crew of two, the pilot and a co-pilot/systems operator, the Griffin could carry up to six people or 1,500 pounds of cargo in the rear compartment. An electric winch controlled from the cockpit allowed for the movement of equipment or personnel to and from the rear compartment without having to land.

One of the major differences between the Griffin and the other police helicopters that had preceded it was that the Griffin was a full bore gunship. Along with the usual police missions of search and rescue, evacuating casualties and serving as a patrol car in the sky, the Griffins could be armed with a variety of weapons in its nose turret and on the stub wing weapons hard points.

Normally, a 40mm grenade launcher was fitted to the 360 degree turret that could select from a variety of ammunition to include flash-bang grenades, tear gas bombs, smoke cartridges, or a low fragmentation HE round. Also, a select

7

fire, 7.62mm Chain Gun or the bigger 25mm version was mounted in the turret alongside the grenade launcher.

Unlike the earlier electric motor driven, multi-barrel Vulcans and Mini-guns, the Chain Gun was a single barrel weapon that could be fired at a variable rate ranging from a single shot to 900 rounds per minute. The rate of fire was controlled by the gunner's right trigger. A light touch fired a single shot, but laying back on the trigger unleashed the full power of the weapon. All of the weapons systems were controlled by the co-pilot/systems operator, but could be fired by the pilot if necessary.

As they flew through the cloudless, china blue sky, Wolff briefed the Mexican pilot on the Griffin's sophisticated sensor and weapons controls.

"The weapons controls are easy," Wolff said as he activated the targeting sensors. "If you can look at it, you can shoot at it and you'll hit it. See the crosshairs in the visor?"

Cuervo nodded.

"The weapons targeting systems are slaved to the helmets," Wolff continued. "And the visor serves as the weapons sight. It gives you the range as well as your weapons and ammunition status. Put the crosshairs on a target and take up the slack on the right trigger."

The Mexican turned his head, "I see it," he said. "It's reading '4,284 meters. Weapons on standby. Full ammunition load'."

"That's all there is to it," Wolff grinned. "When the sight says it's in range, you just shoot at it and you hit it. It's as simple as that."

"And," Wolff continued his briefing. "Not only can we dish it out, we can take it too. Usually, it's not too hard to knock down a chopper, but with all the armor we're carrying, these things are flying tanks. We have back up flight controls, self sealing fuel tanks and the turbine nacelles are armored against ground fire."

The pilot reached up and tapped the canopy in front of him. "This is bulletproof Lexan and your seat is a Kevlar resin composite like the skin all around the cockpit. We're pretty much immune to anything up to and including 7.62mm armor-piercing stuff.''

"But the best part of this whole package, though," Wolff went on to explain, "is the sensors. Without them, we might as well just be flying old Jet Rangers with guns. I've got threat sensors that can pick up both radar and laser designators. I've got doppler radar I can use to track movement on the ground. All of this sensor data feeds into our helmet displays and digital readouts and we can see it on either our helmet visors or the heads up displays.''

Lt. Cuervo studied the grids, following the commentary.

"Then for night flying," the pilot continued. "I've got both active infrared and light intensifying systems that let me see in the dark under any conditions. Then, when I plug that data into the terrain-following radar navigation and mapping system, I can tell where I am at all times day or night and under any kind of weather conditions.''

"The last trick this thing can do," Wolff said, "is what we call the taclink mode. This allows the digital data from both the computer and the sensors to be sent between the chopper and a ground station as well being sent to other Griffins.''

"If I'm taclinked to another Griffin when I make an attack," Wolff explained. "I can send all of my target and sensor data to him and he can 'see' everything I'm doing on his tactical monitor. That way, if I fuck up and get blasted out of the sky, the other pilot will know what I did wrong and he can plan his attack differently.''

"That won't help you much," Cuervo said.

"No," Wolff grinned. "But it keeps two of us from making the same stupid mistake.''

Wolff reached out to the control panel and flipped a switch, "Also, by using our satellite communications system, I can send my attack data to any base in the country if I'm flying alone and far from home.''

Suddenly, the monitor screen lit up and the radio burst into life. "Dragon One Zero, Dragon One Zero, this is

Dragon Control. I have priority traffic for you, come in please."

Wolff keyed his throat mike. "This is One Zero, go ahead."

The distinctive raspy voice of TPF Sergeant Ruby Jenkins, the voice of Dragon Control at the Denver Western Regional Headquarters of the TPF, brought Mugabe out of his nap with a start. He scrambled up behind the pilot's seat to see what in the hell was going on.

"This is Dragon Control, where in the hell have you been, One Zero? I've been trying to contact you for the last ten minutes."

"This is One Zero," Wolff answered. "Sorry 'bout that, Mom. I've been showing my guest how the Griffin's systems work and I guess that I had the taclink shut down. What's up?"

"This is Control. We have picked up a broadcast from a terrorist group threatening to blow up an American offshore oil rig in the Gulf of California. Command One wants you and One Three at that location ASAP. How copy?"

"One Zero, good copy. Where are we going?"

"This is Dragon Control. The Rio Tina platform at coordinates three-four-eight, seven-nine-four. Go Code Twenty. How copy."

"One Zero, good copy," Wolff said as he quickly plugged the oil rig's coordinates into his navigation computer and called up the map on his tactical screen.

"Looks like it's about forty miles from here," he told Mugabe. "And a couple miles out into the Gulf."

The pilot keyed his mike. "Control, this is One Zero. We're not too far from there and are on our way now."

"Control, keep me informed."

"Dragon One Three," Wolff radioed over to Steve Browning, the pilot of the other Griffin flying in formation with him. "This is One Zero, turn the wick up and follow me."

Mom had said Code Twenty and that meant scramble, get there as fast as he could. Wolff's right hand twisted the

10

throttle on the collective control stick all the way against the stop. The Griffin quickly accelerated, leaving the second chopper behind.

"Hey, Wolfman!" Browning called as he banked his ship around to fall in behind Wolff's machine. "Where the hell are we going?"

"Just follow me, Brownie, we're making a house call."

Chapter 2

Baja California

As Dragon One Zero sped for the oil rig, Mugabe crowded into the cockpit behind the gunner's seat. "Quick!" he told the Mexican pilot. "Let me in there!"

Lieutenant Cuervo unbuckled his shoulder harness and wiggled out of the left seat. As soon as he was clear, Mugabe squeezed past him, lowered himself into his office and buckled in. He never felt completely comfortable in the air unless he was at the controls of his weapons.

"What's our ETA?" the gunner snapped, his fingers flying as he activated the targeting radar, turned on the sensors and armed the turret weapons.

"Eighteen minutes," Wolff responded.

Cuervo had also been listening in on the radio traffic and he realized that he could probably help the chopper cops. "If you can give me a clear channel," he said. "I can contact my people and have someone waiting for us on the ground in case we need help."

"What frequency you need?" Wolff asked.

"One one two three UHF."

The pilot quickly switched the UHF radio over to the Mexican channel. "It's set. Go."

11

Cuervo keyed the throat mike on his helmet and in rapid-fire Spanish made contact with the Mexican Federal Police station closest to the oil rig. They had already been notified of the terrorists' threat and that the Griffins would be operating in their area. The station commander was moving a ground unit in to secure the oil rig's supply boat dock at Rio Tina. Cuervo advised him that he was on board one of the American helicopters and could coordinate the operation from the air.

The Treaty of Bogota signed at the conclusion of the Nicaraguan War of 1992 had set the framework for international cooperation between Western Hemispheric nations to combat international terrorist activities. The treaty set guidelines for the police and internal security forces of all of the North and South American nations to freely assist one another against terrorist threats without having to get the politicians involved. It allowed operations like this to be coordinated quickly when fast action could possibly short-stop a potential tragedy.

"Wolff," Cuervo reported. "The Federales are already on their way to the boat dock, but they say that they have had no contact with the oil platform since the terrorists made the broadcast."

"What's the oil company's frequency?" Wolff asked.

"One oh two point six FM."

Wolff switched over to that channel and keyed his throat mike. "Calling Rio Tina platform, this is the United States Tactical Police Force helicopter Dragon One Zero. We are enroute to your location, come in please."

The pilot repeated his message three times, but there was no answer. "Shit!"

"Heads up!" he warned Mugabe as the top of the oil drilling tower came in view. "There it is!"

A little over two miles from the shore, the oil platform was a two hundred meter square steel island in the Gulf of California supported by four legs anchoring it to the bottom. The drilling rig itself sat in one corner surrounded by machinery and over half of the platform was taken up with

12

the crew's living quarters. The rest of the rig was crowded with the huge valves and pipes needed to transfer the crude oil to the tanker ships.

"I've got an aircraft at eleven o'clock!" Mugabe called out, looking up from his screen.

"I got him!" Wolff replied, spotting the speck in the sky racing away from the oil platform, a helicopter going balls-out. He flipped over to the international emergency and rescue frequency and keyed his throat mike.

"Unknown aircraft at three thousand feet and heading south on a bearing of one niner six," he radioed. "This is the United States Tactical Police. Return to the Rio Tina oil platform and land. Over."

There was no response. Wolff repeated the message, but there was still no answer.

"That's got to be the bad guys," Mugabe said. "If they were clean, they'd answer."

The pilot switched back to the chopper-to-chopper channel. "One Three," he radioed to the other Griffin. "This is the Wolfman, I'm going after the suspect aircraft. We have negative contact with the oil rig, so I want you to check it out and see what in the hell is going on down there."

"One Three, copy." Browning radioed back as he broke formation and banked away to head down for the helipad on the platform.

The chopper was two hundred meters away from the drilling tower when a boiling ball of angry red and black flame shot up into the air, instantly engulfing the entire platform in a fiery inferno. The explosive blast slapped Browning's Griffin out of the sky as though it had been hit by a giant fly swatter. It fell as if there was no one at the controls.

"Oh Sweet Jesus!" Mugabe said a second before the shock wave hit their own ship.

The blast of heated air against the bottoms of the rotor blades canceled the lift and unloaded the rotor head. The turbines screamed in over-rev and Wolff suddenly had both his hands full trying to keep his own machine from following

13

the other ship into an uncontrollable spin. Slamming the cyclic control into the upper left corner and stomping down on the left rudder pedal as he chopped the throttle, Wolff laid the Griffin over on her left side and sent her into a sharp dive toward the water.

As soon as he felt the rotor blades hit undisturbed air, his right hand hauled up on the collective and he twisted the throttle back up to ninety percent. The blades caught lift again and Wolff banked One Zero around just in time to see the spiraling One Three splash into the Gulf several hundred meters away from the burning oil rig.

The doomed chopper disappeared under the waves, shattering the spinning main rotor blades when they hit the water. A second later, the Griffin bobbed back up to the surface and settled down, the fuselage floating half out of the water like a sinking boat. Flaming debris slashed down into the water around One Three, churning the calm surface of the Gulf of California into a froth. Burning oil shooting out from the ruptured oil lines on the platform quickly spread toward the downed ship.

Wolff keyed his throat mike and flicked on the external speakers. "Brownie! Simpson! Get out of there!"

There was no answer, but Wolff saw the gunner's door open and watched as Simpson jumped out into the water. The gunner quickly swam around the nose of the ship and pulled the pilot's door open. Reaching in, he unbuckled Browning's shoulder harness and pulled the pilot out. It looked like Brownie was unconscious as Simpson swam away from the sinking chopper with the pilot in his arms.

"Cuervo!" Wolff called back over the intercom. "Open up the right side door back there, I'm going to lower the winch. As soon as the rescue collar reaches them, stand by to help them get into it!"

The Mexican cop unlatched the door and slid the winch arm out into the rotor blast. Wolff hit the switch and a rescue collar started down on the end of the steel cable. Maneuvering the Griffin above the two men in the water, he came down in a hover until the ship was just a few meters

14

off the wave tops. The circular pattern of the rotor blast flattened the waves and the rescue collar dropped into the center of the circle inches away from the two men.

Simpson grabbed at the collar, but he seemed to be having difficulty with his free arm. He drew it to him, but couldn't get it around the unconscious pilot's chest.

"Simpson!" Wolff called down over the loudspeaker mounted in the ship's belly. "Inflate Brownie's life jacket and take the collar yourself! We'll get him next!"

The gunner pulled at the tab on the shoulder of the unconscious pilot's flight suit. It inflated into a life jacket that held Brownie's head and shoulders well out of the water. He then released him and grabbed onto the rescue collar with his good arm.

Wolff hit the winch switch and quickly reeled in the wounded man. Cuervo helped the gunner into the back of the Griffin, stripped the rescue collar from him and dropped it back down over the side again.

"Lower away!" Cuervo called up to the pilot. "I'm going down after the other one!"

Without waiting for Wolff to answer, Cuervo stepped out into the rotor blast and climbed down onto the chopper's skid, trailing the intercom cord behind him. Hanging onto the skid strut with one arm, he reached down and tried to grab onto the unconscious pilot.

"I can't reach him!" he called up to Wolff. "Bring the chopper down lower!"

Wolff eased down on the collective and the skids dropped into the water, threatening to draw the ship under. As the pilot balanced the hovering Griffin mere inches above the water, Cuervo held onto the skid strut with one hand and was able to reach out and grab Browning by the back of his inflated flight suit.

"Got him!"

The Mexican pilot hauled the unconscious man out of the water and lifted him up onto the skid. He quickly slipped the rescue collar down over his chest and secured it. Wolff took up the slack on the cable, lifting Browning up to the

15

open door. Cuervo climbed back up into the ship and pulled the pilot safely inside.

"He's breathing!" the Mexican cop reported. "And nothing seems to be broken, but you'd better get him on shore. My people will have a medic with them."

"On the way."

Dense clouds of billowing greasy black smoke rose from the blazing oil rig as Wolff lifted the chopper up into the air and sped for the dock.

Wolff flared out sharply and landed the Griffin in the dirt parking lot at the end of the dock. Cuervo jumped down and ran over to the officer in charge of the Mexican police unit. Like he had promised, a Federale medic was on hand and the Mexican pilot got him to attend to the injured chopper cops immediately.

Browning had come to and was trying to sit up, but the medic made him lie on the floor of the Griffin while he checked him out. Except for a bruise on the side of his head where he had slammed into the cockpit frame in the crash, he was okay. Simpson had a dislocated shoulder, but was otherwise just fine. The medic strapped them in and covered them with blankets until they could be transported to the hospital.

While the medic saw to the two chopper cops, Wolff and Mugabe shut down the Griffin and went to talk to the Mexican officer. He reported that when he had arrived, he had discovered that the terrorists had brought the five man crew of the oil rig there and tied them up before putting the explosive charges in place. While Wolff questioned the five men from the oil rig about what had happened, Cuervo translated their stories for the Mexican authorities, but the men had little to tell them about the incident.

An hour earlier, an unannounced helicopter had landed on their helipad. When they came out to see who it was, armed men in camouflage uniforms and ski masks had rounded them up and flown them to the dock where they

16

had been tied up. The chopper then went back to the oil platform, stayed for a while, and then flew off right as the Griffins appeared.

They couldn't identify any of their attackers and none of the men had spoken more than curt orders in accented English. They had also never seen the helicopter before and no one had noticed any markings on it.

"We've got fuck-all to go on here," Wolff said, looking out over the water at the blazing oil rig. "The perfect commando raid. Quick in, quick out and leave nothing behind except a real fucking mess to clean up."

"Who do you think could be behind something like this?" Cuervo asked.

Wolff shrugged. "Beats the shit outa me. Could be any number of things from terrorism to a pissed off husband whose wife has been sleeping with one of the crew."

"That's a pretty radical thing to do just because you're pissed off at your wife," Mugabe said.

"Stranger things have happened," Wolff replied. "Remember the guy in Arizona who was taking out armored cars because one of them ran him off the road once?"

When they were on the ground, Wolff made it a practice to always keep the Griffin's radios turned on and switched over to the external microphones so he could monitor any traffic for them.

"This is the Vengeance of God," a heavily accented voice suddenly broke in over the loudspeakers. "The destruction of the Rio Tina oil platform is only the first of the punishments that Allah has ordered for the Western infidels who supported the barbaric Jewish attacks on the nations of Islam."

"Oh Jesus," Wolff spun around and raced for the chopper. "Not this shit again!"

Mugabe was hot on his heels.

17

Chapter 3

Rio Tina, Baja California

It had been several years since the Arabic world had last exploded in a short-lived orgy of terrorism during the aftermath of the last war with Israel. Most Americans thought that anti-Semitism as an excuse for international terrorism was finally a thing of the past.

The short, but devastating 5th Arab-Israeli war of 1992 saw the first use of tactical nuclear weapons since World War II, when the Syrians launched one of their nuclear-tipped, Red Chinese rockets at Tel Aviv. No one ever knew for certain if the missile had been launched on orders of the Syrian leaders or by accident. But, regardless of the reason the rocket had been fired, a quarter of the city was destroyed and thousands of people killed in the attack.

The Israelis instantly retaliated. Not only did they launch their secret nuclear arsenal at the seats of government in Baghdad, Teheran, Tripoli and the PLO headquarters in the Bekaa Valley, but they also targeted the major oil production centers in Libya, Iran and Syria.

When the missiles started flying, most of the other Arabic nations wisely stayed out of it. But the Egyptians felt that they had to make a gesture of solidarity with their Arab brothers and launched a massive air strike against Israel. The Israelis were in no mood to play with them. After destroying the Egyptian air fleet with nuclear air-to-air missiles, more nuclear-tipped missiles took out their oil fields as well as their major military installations.

When the war ended the next day, Libya, Iran, Syria, Egypt and the Palestinians had been destroyed as military powers for the next hundred years. The survivors also found that their economies were completely bankrupt.

When the stunned Arab nations dug out from under the radioactive rubble, they discovered that over half of the OPEC oil fields had been contaminated by the Israeli nuclear strikes and could not be worked. Even some of the oil fields that had not been directly hit by the nuclear strikes had also been contaminated by the underground transmission of radioactivity. Even the economies of the untouched Arab oil producing nations promptly collapsed and the Arab world exploded in an orgy of violence.

Most of the violence was internal, Arab against Arab, as old tribal and religious hatreds re-emerged in the grim battle for survival. The violent Shiite sect of Islam vanished under the swords of the Sunni Moslems. National boundaries shifted weekly as old tribal conflicts raged anew. It was a great time of killing.

The western world briefly panicked at the loss of the Arab oil production, but then plunged into the exploration of new sources of petroleum. Within a year, massive new oil deposits had been discovered in South America and the Gulf of Mexico. These finds, coupled with increased Russian production in Siberia, made up for the lost Arab oil and the western world settled down.

The Arab world had also appeared to settle down when they discovered that without the financial support of the western nations, they were all going to starve to death. Moderate Arabs quickly eliminated the radicals and peace finally came to the Middle East.

Now however, it looked like the old specter of Arab terrorism had risen from the grave.

When Wolff reached the chopper, he glanced at the radio readout and saw that the terrorist's transmission was coming in over the international emergency channel. He slipped his flight helmet down over his head and cut off the external speakers.

"We will continue to punish infidel petroleum facilities," the accented voice continued over his headphones. "Until the capitalist oil companies confess their guilt and make repatriations for the damage they did to the oil fields of the nations of Islam. Allah will have his vengeance."

Wolff quickly switched over to the Dragon Control frequency and accessed the satellite link communication band so he could transmit all the way back to Denver.

"Dragon Control, this is One Zero," he radioed. "We're getting a terrorist transmission on the international emergency channel. Are you picking up this guy?"

"Copy, One Zero" came Mom's calm voice. "I'm taping him and I'm on the satcom link right now to see if I can get a trace on his location."

To help facilitate better police communications nationwide, NASA had used the space shuttle to launch a special satellite into a stationary orbit a thousand miles above the United States. By linking into this communications satellite, police forces all over the United States could talk to one another as easily as using the telephone to call across town. The satellite could also be used to pinpoint radio transmitters anywhere in the country as well. Usually, this feature was used in rescue work to locate emergency transmitters from downed aircraft, but it could also be used to find this kind of transmitter.

After a short moment, Mom came back on the air. "One Zero, this is Dragon Control," she radioed. "I've got a fix on that transmitter. It's at zero-eight-seven, four-nine-three. How copy?"

Mugabe had slid into his seat and had called up his navigational map. He quickly plotted the coordinates, a spot in the mountains right in the middle of Baja California and about fifty miles inland from the Gulf of California. He shot Wolff a thumbs up.

"This is One Zero, we have good copy," the pilot radioed back. "I'll pass this information on to the Mexican authorities."

"This is Dragon Control, Command One has already been in contact with the Mexican government and he advises that you have been placed on detached duty with the

Federales to assist their investigation of this incident. You are to report to the Mexican police airfield at Santa Rosilia for further instructions.''

"One Zero, good copy," Wolff answered. "Do you have any more traffic for me?''

"This is Dragon Control," Mom replied. "That's a negative. Good luck and good hunting.''

Wolff pulled his helmet off and laid it in his seat. "Looks like we'll have time to sample a little more of Lieutenant Cuervo's favorite family recipe after all," he told his gunner with a grin. "We've been loaned to the Federales for a while.''

Mugabe grimaced. "Damn, I still haven't recovered from the tequila we drank last night.''

"You've just got to get in better shape, Mojo," Wolff laughed. "The chopper cops have a reputation to uphold and you're letting us down. What will the Federales think if you let them drink us under the table?''

"Machismo, right?''

"Right," Wolff grinned. "I'll go find Arturo and we'll get going.''

It was a short flight to the Mexican Police airstrip right outside the little town of Santa Rosilia mid-way up the western coast of Baja California. The landing field was little more than a small dirt strip with two wooden hangars, a spindly control tower and an adobe police station headquarters building.

Cuervo had radioed ahead and an ambulance was waiting to take Browning and Simpson to the town's modern hospital to be checked over by a doctor in case they had internal injuries that the medic at the dock might have missed.

After the ambulance took the two chopper cops away, Wolff and Mugabe followed Cuervo into the operations office to meet the Mexican Police officer in command of the unit that would accompany them to the suspected terrorist hideout in the mountains. There was only one unarmed

21

helicopter based at this small airstrip, so the commander had to request more choppers from other Federale units and that was going to take a little time.

While the Mexicans assembled their forces, Wolff and Mugabe thoroughly checked over their chopper to see if she had sustained any damage from the explosion, but to their relief, there was none. They were just snapping the last of the inspection panels back in place when Cuervo came out of the police headquarters building and walked over to them.

"We can't get all of the helicopters until tomorrow," he said. "So you will have to spend the night here, but I think that I can find good accommodations for you in the town. Santa Rosilia is small, but I can find a nice cantina for you with clean rooms."

"Anyplace is fine with me," Wolff grinned. "As long as they serve tequila."

Cuervo laughed and threw his arms open wide. "Senores," he said. "This is Mexico you are in. Of course you can have tequila, all you can drink."

Mugabe groaned. "Here we go again."

"Don't worry, ole buddy," Wolff said clapping his hand on Mugabe's shoulder. "I'll make sure that you get tucked in tonight."

"That's what I'm afraid of."

Rick Wolff and Jumal Mugabe went back all the way to the inception of the Tac Force Dragon Flight. They had both been in the first Griffin helicopter conversion class and had been assigned to fly together at the start of the weapons phase of the training.

At first, Wolff hadn't known what to make of the muscular, black cop with the shaved head, the single gold earring and the jive ass attitude. But after the first day on the gunnery range he knew that he was working with a master of aerial gunnery, a real left seat ace.

That night the two men discovered that they had quite a bit in common, most of it revolved around their love of flying. The burly gunner had flown in choppers for several of the government's secret armies as well as for the CIA

22

and DEA. Mugabe related how he had finally gotten combat out of his system when he had stopped a bullet in the jungle and had tried his hand at civilian life for a while. That, however, quickly proved to be too boring for him, so he immediately signed up for the Tac Force when they started recruiting gunship crews.

Wolff had not been able to fly in any of the recent brush wars of the last decade. He did his time as a hot rock air show and racing pilot who had restored a World War II vintage F4U-5 Corsair fighter to play around with. Mugabe immediately volunteered his services if Wolff needed mechanic work done on the plane. Among his many talents, Mugabe was also an ace aircraft mechanic and he enjoyed working on old warbirds, particularly fighter planes.

When the two men graduated from the Griffin flight school, Wolff was ranked as the top pilot and Mugabe as the top gunner so it was only natural that they be assigned to fly together as the hottest gunship team in the TPF. The "Top Gun" trophies they racked up at each year's Tac Force gunnery competition was proof that they were well matched in the air.

Not only did they fly together every day, they also spent most of their off-duty time together as well. Most cops' friends are always other cops. No one else could understand what they did as well.

Arturo Cuervo was as good as his word; the small cantina he drove Wolff and Mugabe to in the small town was clean and the food was good. To prove that the tequila was drinkable, he stayed to have a few drinks with the two Americans.

"If I remember right," Wolff said. "You told me that your family was in agriculture."

"Yes," Cuervo answered. "They have farm land and orchards in the interior, why?"

"Well," Wolff asked, pointing to the half empty bottle of

23

tequila on their table. "Why is it that I see your family name on so many of these?"

Cuervo grinned and poured himself another shot. "Well," he said, "it's a long story. It goes back to my great-grandfather and his brother Jose, how do you say it? The black sheep of the family. He was very fond of tequila and it is said that he complained to the distiller in his town one day about the quality of the tequila he produced. The man laughed at him and challenged him to make better."

Cuervo took a small drink from his glass. "And, as they say, the rest is history."

"Here's to Jose," Wolff said raising his own glass. "Long may his name be known."

"Hear! Hear!" Mugabe added, sipping his beer.

Chapter 4

Santa Rosilia, Mexico

When Lieutenant Cuervo drove Wolff and Mugabe out to the small air strip early the next morning, the chopper cops saw that the Federales had gathered an impressive aerial fleet for the morning's operation.

Three twenty-year-old UH-1N Hueys were on hand to carry the troops who would conduct the ground search. Next to the Hueys sat two slightly newer AH-1S Cobra gunships that would help the Griffin with the ground support tasks. Though they were older aircraft, the Mexican ships looked to have been extremely well maintained. Their paint was fresh, their canopies were polished and their red, white and blue triangular national markings proudly gleamed in the tropical sun.

A platoon of Mexican assault police lounged in the shade

of the hangar waiting to board the choppers for the assault. Dressed in desert camouflage SWAT uniforms and armed with late model weapons, the Federales had that casual, but hard eyed look of true professionals. Since the early 1990s, Mexico had been allied with the United States in the fight against drug terrorism and the Federales had had a lot of practice with this kind of operation. There was no doubt in Wolff's mind that they could hold up their end of the stick if things got rough out there today.

The three cops went on into the operations shack to meet the Mexican pilots who would be flying the choppers outside. After a last minute map check of their operational area and assignment of the radio call signs, they headed outside to board their ships.

It was show time.

Cuervo climbed into Wolff's Griffin and settled down in the foldout jump seat behind the pilot. Although all of the Mexican pilots and most of the ground leaders spoke English, Cuervo was going to act as the coordinator for the mission to prevent any misunderstandings. When you're getting shot at, it's no time to have to stop and try to figure out what someone just told you to do.

As soon as Cuervo reported that the Federale chopper pilots had finished their pre-flight checks, Wolff triggered the switch to his throat mike. "Tequila Flight," he radioed to them. "This is One Zero, start up."

As the rogers came in from the five other pilots, Mugabe began the turbine startup checklist. Wolff's gloved fingers flew over the Griffin's switches and controls as he called out each item to his co-pilot.

"Battery, on. Internal power, on. Inverter switch, off. RPM warning light, on. Fuel, both main and start, on. RPM governor, decrease."

Mugabe looked over his shoulder to check both sides of the ship. "Rotor, clear. Light it!"

Reaching down with his right hand to the collective control stick, Wolff twisted the throttle open to Flight Idle and pulled the starting trigger. In the rear of the bird, the portside GE T-700 turbine burst into life with a screeching whine and a smell of burned kerosene. Over their heads, the forty foot main rotor slowly began to turn, moving faster and faster. As soon as the portside turbine was running at forty percent RPM, Wolff switched over to the starboard turbine and fired it up.

While the turbine RPMs built up and the rotor blades came up to speed, the pilot held the throttle at flight idle and watched the exhaust gas temperature and RPM gauges closely. Everything was in the green.

He twisted the throttle all the way up against the stop. The jet whine built to a bone-shaking scream as the twin turbines ran up all the way to 6,000 RPM. Everything was still in the green.

He flipped the RPM governor switch to increase and the turbines screamed even higher at 6700 RPMs. Everything was still green.

Wolff backed off on the throttle, and waited as the Mexican choppers called their status in to him. When all five ships reported that they were go, Wolff gave the word to take off. As the flight leader, he taxied the Griffin out onto the runway first and the other machines fell in line right behind him.

Lining up with the end of the runway, Wolff twisted the throttle to full RPM, eased up on the collective control and nudged forward on the cyclic stick. Tail high, the Griffin started down the runway. As soon as the airspeed came up, he hauled up on the collective, pulling maximum pitch to the rotor blades, and One Zero zoomed up into the clear sky. The Mexican choppers followed him as quickly as they could.

As soon as everyone was airborne, the flight formed up in a vee formation with the Griffin leading, the two Mexican Cobras on each side and the three Huey slicks trailing behind. To keep from running away from the slower Hueys, Wolff kept his airspeed down to just over a hundred miles an hour. The Cobras could have kept pace with the Griffin's

26

normal 175 mile an hour cruising speed, but the loaded down old Hueys could never have stayed with the gunships.

Wolff kept the formation close to the ground as they flew over the barren, sunbaked mountains of central Baja California. He had no way of knowing if the terrorists had radar and anti-aircraft defenses guarding their mountain hideout, but it never hurt to be cautious.

"What're the Rules of Engagement around here?" Mugabe asked Cuervo as they approached the target area.

There were three levels of the Rules of Engagement governing the use of deadly force in the TPF, ROE Alpha, Bravo and Charlie. Alpha allowed the use of weapons only to save a life, Bravo allowed the Tac Cops to shoot back at anyone who shot at them and Charlie was a shoot on sight order that was only authorized in extreme emergencies.

Cuervo shrugged. "We are not very formal about that around here," he said with a smile. "If you think that we are in danger today, shoot first. We will sort out the bodies later."

Mugabe grinned. "I can live with that," he said. "That's what we call ROE Charlie in the Tac Force and we don't get to use it much."

The gunner reached forward and flicked on the arming switches to the weapons in the nose turret and dialed in the standard ammunition feed. Since he didn't know what kind of defense the terrorists might have, he also went to Full Defensive mode and switched on the "Mirror Skin" system of the Griffin.

Mirror Skin was a counter-measure designed to protect the Griffin from laser guided anti-aircraft missiles by changing the refractive index of the chopper's skin. A minute amount of electric current was sent through the chopper's outer skin and excited the di-electric molecules of the special dark blue paint increasing its refractive index by five thousand percent. This scattered the light beam and made it difficult for a laser to lock onto the chopper. From the ground, it made the chopper look like it had been coated with a solid sheet of bright blue mirrored glass.

The Mirror Skin made it difficult for a laser guided missile to achieve a lock-on, but it was not complete insurance against their being shot down by a shoulder fired missile. Many anti-aircraft missiles also had a secondary infrared guidance system backing up the laser. Their chopper was not fitted with the Black Hole IR suppression kits on the turbine exhausts, so they were still vulnerable to someone shooting at them with a heat seeking missile.

"We're supposed to be on a vacation," Mugabe growled. "If I had known that we were going to get into a pissing contest down here, I'd have talked Red into fitting the IR kits before we left."

"Just be glad that we were fully armed." Wolff said. "Otherwise, we'd be orbiting off to the side or playing troop carrier today. The Mexicans don't use our brand of forty mm or twenty-five mm."

"Thank God for small favors," Mugabe replied. "You know how I hate to sit on the sidelines when all the fun's happening."

Just as any off duty policeman always carries a loaded sidearm, everywhere the Griffins of Dragon Flight went they were always topped off with a full ammunition load for their on board weapons.

"Heads up," Wolff said, checking the readout on his terrain following radar. "It should be just behind that next ridge line."

Cuervo quickly relayed that information to the Mexican pilots and the three troop carrying Hueys dropped back a little farther to give the Griffin and the Cobra gunships first crack at the bad guys.

"There it is," Cuervo said, pointing to the cluster of small, weathered buildings in a narrow, isolated valley off to their right.

"Doesn't look like anyone's at home," Mugabe said, his sensors rapidly scanning the barren terrain for any sign of life, biological or electronic.

"Don't take your thumb off the button," Wolff cautioned, banking the Griffin over to take advantage of what cover he could get from the terrain. "They could be keeping under cover down there. What are you getting on the sensors?"

"Not much," the gunner answered. "No doppler, no radar and the only IR readings I'm getting are from large stationary masses. Probably steel baking in the sun."

"No radio?"

"Nada," Mugabe shook his head slightly. "All frequency bands are clear, both AM and FM."

"Shit!"

Flanked by the two Mexican Cobras, the Griffin made two lower passes over the small camp, her sensors seeking any kind of life on the ground. But there was nothing. According to the readouts from the Griffin's full battery of sensors, the suspected terrorist camp was every bit as deserted as it looked to the naked eye.

"There's no sign of anyone down there," Wolff told Cuervo. "Why don't you tell the Hueys to set down and take a look to see if the bad guys left anything behind."

The Mexican cop quickly gave the order and the three Hueys swooped in for a landing under the watchful eyes of the three gunships. The twenty desert camouflaged Federales stormed out of the ships and cautiously started searching the buildings one by one.

"They say that the camp is deserted," Cuervo reported a few minutes later.

"I'm going to set down," Wolff said. "Tell one of the Cobras to stay up there and cover us just in case."

Wolff set his gunship down with the nose turret facing the buildings and Mugabe stayed at his weapons controls while the pilot opened his door and jumped down to the ground. Drawing his Glock 10mm pistol, Wolff flicked the safety off before walking too far away from the protection of his ship's guns.

The deserted camp looked like a set for a Road Warrior movie. Sun-bleached siding on the buildings, broken windows, doors hanging askew on their hinges. A battered derelict pickup truck sat on its axles behind the largest building.

It didn't look like anyone had been here for years. Wolff turned and motioned for Mugabe to join him.

"You sure this is the right place, Mojo?" he asked the gunner.

"These are the coordinates Mom gave me," Mugabe shrugged. "Maybe she didn't get a good fix on the transmitter."

"Do you want me to tell her that you said that?"

"Not really," Mugabe grinned. Ruby Jenkins took great pride in her ability to use the high tech gadgets of the TPF and she would not be pleased to hear that she had sent them to the wrong place.

"We'd better help Cuervo's boys check this out thoroughly before I get on the horn back to Denver."

"Yeah, let's do it."

The two chopper cops fanned out to help the Mexicans with the search. They went through each one of the buildings again, checked the derelict vehicles and piles of trash lying around. They even turned over empty oil drums and looked inside them. There was absolutely nothing.

Wolff spotted what looked like another collection of junk several meters away from the edge of the cluster of buildings and walked over to check it out too. When he reported their failure, he wanted to be able to say that they had searched absolutely everything. When he got within a few meters, he saw the characteristic round, flat shape of a small dish antenna and this was the last place in the world that anyone would have cable TV.

"Yo! Mojo! Arturo!" Wolff called out. "Quick! Over here!"

The two cops came running.

"What you got?" Mugabe asked.

Wolff pointed to the small dish antenna connected to a small box half hidden in the trash. It had to be a powerful radio transmitter.

"I'll be a son of a bitch," Mugabe exploded, kneeling down to get a better look. "They've suckered us. That's a fucking retrans setup."

30

"A what?" Cuervo frowned.

"A retransmission station," Wolff explained. "It picks up a radio transmission from somewhere else and re-broadcasts it from here. And, if the first transmission is on a tight enough beam, it can't be traced to its origin."

"You mean that you can't find where the original terrorist broadcast came from?" Cuervo asked.

"That's about it," Mugabe said grimly. "Whoever did this was fucking with us. He knew that we could get a fix on his broadcast and did this so we'd waste our time looking for him here while he gets away clean."

"Collect up this gear," Wolff said. "While I go back and get on the horn to Denver. They need to know about this ASAP so they can get out a terrorist alert."

"Yeah," Mugabe agreed. "While we're screwing around here, these guys could be half a continent away."

"They always were somewhere else," Wolff said grimly. "We got suckered."

"*Mierda!*" Cuervo said.

Chapter 5

Western Region TPF Headquarters, Denver

At first light the next morning, Wolff and Mugabe took off from the Mexican airstrip at Santa Rosilia. As soon as they were in the air, Wolff turned the wick up and shortly after noon they had arrived back at the TPF Western Region headquarters in Denver. Wolff flared the Griffin out for a landing and taxied the gunship over to its place on the flight line. When they stepped out onto the cold, wet tarmac, they found Red Larson bundled in a fur-lined parka waiting for them.

Larson was the Dragon Flight Maintenance Officer and the Crew Chief for Dragon One Zero. Red was a big, burly man who looked every one of his fifty-odd years, but age had not slowed him down all that much. The remnants of his once flaming red hair served as ample warning that he still had a fiery temper.

Red's love affair with helicopters had begun back when he had gone to Vietnam as a nineteen year old chopper mechanic in the Air Cav. When he had gotten out of the Army at the end of the long war, he had taken a job working on police choppers and now, almost thirty years later, he was still in love with rotary wing flying machines.

Because of his well-earned reputation and years of experience working with police choppers, when the Griffin was on the drawing boards, Red had been called in as a consultant to advise the Bell design team as to what a real police helicopter should be like. Since he had had a hand in creating the final design, Red considered the Griffins to be his children. Woe be unto any young hot shot pilot who abused one of his birds, particularly anyone who crashed one of his Griffins without a damned good excuse.

"Red, my man," Mugabe greeted him, eyeing his warm parka as he stepped out into the cold Denver weather. "Where do I get me one of them coats?"

Mojo never missed an opportunity to use black street language when he had an audience. The only son of sixties civil rights black activists, Mugabe had to put up with a lot of good-natured ribbing from his fellow officers about his African name. To pay them back, he played the role to the hilt every chance that he had.

"Join the Air Force," Red growled around the dead cigar butt clamped between his teeth. "I understand that you jokers left Dragon One Three in a hundred feet of water."

"Hey! Wait a minute, Chief," Wolff said. "You need to talk to Officer Browning about that. He was the guy flying that thing, not me."

"He's still in the hospital, so I'm talking to you," Red said, his finger stabbing Wolff in the chest. "And you were the flight leader who left one of your aircraft under a hundred feet of salt water, right?"

"Actually, Chief," Wolff said, "It's more like a hundred and twenty feet. But, don't you worry, the oil company has a barge and crane on the way to recover it for you."

Red spat a piece of tobacco onto the tarmac. It steamed in the cool mountain air. "Are they going to dry it out and fly it back here for me too?"

"They said that they could get it to the dock at Rio Tina, but that you'd have to pick it up from there."

"That's fucking outstanding," Red said. "Do you know what salt water does to the electronics of a Griffin?"

Wolff got a boyish, innocent look on his face. "No, Chief, I don't," he admitted. "But I've got a feeling that you're about to tell me all about it."

Red took the cigar out of his mouth and looked Wolff right in the eyes for a long moment. He spat and shoved the cigar back into his mouth. "Buzz left word with me that he wants to see you two cowboys the moment you show up, so I'll finish this little conversation with you later."

"What's he want?" Wolff asked.

Red shrugged. "It ain't my day to advise him, so I don't know. It probably has something to do with your losing one of my birds though."

"We'll stop by and see him after we get cleaned up," Wolff said, turning to go.

"He told me you'd say that,' Red growled. "And he told me to impress upon you two that he wants to see you right-fucking-now."

"Okay, okay," the pilot said. "Keep your pants on, we're going."

Wolff and Mugabe walked into the operations room and were immediately spotted by TPF Sergeant Ruby Jenkins, the brains and voice of Dragon Control, the dispatch center for the Griffins of Dragon Flight. Trim and petite, but as hard as only a woman of her age and experience could be,

Jenkins was affectionately known to the chopper cops as Mom, but no one had ever mistaken her for anyone's mother. She ruled her electronic kingdom with an iron fist and, even when they were on the ground, the pilots knew that when Mom spoke, it was wise to listen carefully.

"He's been waiting for you," she said, not finding it necessary to say who she was referring to. "And you know he doesn't like to wait."

"But we just got in," Wolff protested.

"You've been shooting the shit with Red again, you mean," she answered curtly. "Go on in, I'll let him know that you're finally here."

The two cops walked past her commo console to their CO's office and knocked on the door.

"Come in."

The man behind the cluttered desk, TPF Captain J.D. "Buzz" Corcran, the commander of the Western Region Dragon Flight, was a balding, barrel-chested man in his middle fifties. Corcran had had a long career flying military and police helicopters before he had become the commander of the first TPF Dragon Flight. Even though he was stuck behind a commander's desk, he still considered himself a gunship pilot first and he ran his police unit like the assault helicopter company he had commanded in the 'Nam.

"What can you tell me about that little fiasco down in Mexico?"

"Well sir," Wolff began. "Not much more than you already know. By the time we got to the oil platform, the charges had already been set and it blew up. And you know what happened to Brownie and Simpson. Then, when we hit that transmitter site, no one was home." Wolff shrugged. "There wasn't a hell of a lot we could do."

"I know you guys tried," Buzz said. "But the Tac Force is really under the gun on this one. Another oil rig went up in flames this morning, this time in the Gulf of Mexico. Every senator and congressmen on the oil lobby payroll is screaming his fucking head off about this."

"But it's only been two days since the first attack," Wolff

protested. "We haven't even had time to figure out what's happening yet."

"I know, I know," Buzz said. "But shit like this is supposed to be our reason for existence. We're supposed to be the experts at taking out terrorists, drug armies and street corner maggots with guns. Capitol Hill is in an uproar and the Washington headquarters is taking a lot of flak on this already."

Buzz shook his head. "And you know what happens when the shit hits the fan and the boys in the puzzle palace in DC are standing in the way of it."

"Yes sir," Wolff answered. "Shit rolls downhill and we're at the bottom of the hill."

"At least you have an accurate understanding of the situation," Buzz said dryly.

The Tactical Police Force had been controversial from its very inception in 1996. Back in the mid-1990's, it had become all too apparent that America was losing the war against crime. The efforts of the existing federal law enforcement organizations: the FBI, the Federal Marshals, the DEA, the Sky Marshals, the Customs Police, and the Immigration Service were just not enough to contain the growing crime wave. The primary reason that they had all too often failed was that their efforts were scattered and uncoordinated. But even more important, they were not organized or equipped to deal with criminal gangs that had evolved into small, well armed private armies. The situation had become extremely critical and something new had to be tried.

Initially, there had been a great deal of resistance to the idea of one unified, well equipped Federal police force, particularly from the professional liberal lobby and entrenched corrupt public officials. The political battles on Capitol Hill raged for months, but this was an idea whose time had clearly come. The old methods were not working and the time had come for the government to take control of the country back from the criminal elements.

One of President Bush's last official acts at the end of his second term had been to sign the federal act that created the United States Tactical Police Force. Under the provisions of the law, the TPF was given the authority to preserve the peace and uphold the law anywhere in the fifty United States.

The Tac Force had the authority and they did the job. Maybe too well. They were expected to be supermen. This was one problem, however, that wasn't going to be easy to deal with immediately. Unlike many of the situations they handled in the past, this time they couldn't just fly in with a couple of Griffins and blast the bad guys out of existence. As yet, they didn't have anyone to focus their firepower on and, until they could find out who was behind this latest wave of terrorism, all they could do was sit tight and let the bad guys come to them. It was an extremely frustrating situation for them to be in.

"Washington's got a mission for us," Buzz said. "And I've called a briefing for sixteen hundred hours. So go get cleaned up and I'll see you then."

"Where we going, sir?" Wolff asked.

"You'll hear about it when everybody else does."

"Yes sir." the two cops said in unison.

Wolff and Mugabe walked over to the TPF mess hall for lunch and found their fellow chopper cop Daryl Jennings, the pilot of Dragon One Four, and his co-pilot Sandra Revell sitting at a table by the windows.

"Hi Legs! Gunner!" Wolff grinned as he walked up to their table. "Mind if we join you?"

"Well if it isn't our version of the Blues Brothers, Mojo and his little buddy the Wolfman," Gunner Jennings laughed. "How they hanging, boys? You guys bring anything back from Mexico? Other than a raging case of clap, that is."

"No clap this time," Mojo grinned, pulling a chair back to sit down. "We lucked out, we didn't run into your sister."

36

"Mojo got himself a real nice hat though," Wolff said, ignoring the expression on Jennings' face. "You ought to see it. It makes him look like a pimp in an LA barrio."

"Hey! Lighten up on my sombrero, man," Mugabe replied. "It takes a man with a refined sense of fashion to appreciate finer haberdashery."

The co-pilot looked Wolff up and down, focusing on the well worn World War II leather flying jacket Wolff wore off duty. On one breast was sewn the Dragon Flight patch showing a dragon with a helicopter rotor on his back and a flight helmet on his head. On the other side of the jacket was the insignia of VMF-214 the Marine fighter squadron that had flown the F4U Corsair to fame in the Pacific in World War Two. An American flag was sewn on one shoulder and a "Blood Chit" surrounded by the patches of other police flight units was sewn on the back. Wolff looked every inch the dashing fighter pilot in a B grade World War II flying movie, and that was exactly how he wanted to look.

"But I have a 'refined sense of fashion' ", Wolff protested. "Look, I even added the Federales flight patch to the collection."

"If you two boys are done with your routine," Revell said. "Maybe we can finish our meal?"

Tall, blonde and green eyed, Flight Officer Sandra Revell was a real life version of a glamorous TV woman cop and she was every inch as tough as she was good looking. If she had a fault, it was that she took her job a little too seriously. She knew that she was a knockout and, if she ever forgot, there was no shortage of men who would tell her, particularly the men she worked with.

She worked hard at being a good cop and worked even harder to keep her private life to herself. She never went out with any of the men she worked with and always did her best to keep her on duty relationships strictly professional. But it didn't always work out that way. Like her nickname, Legs.

"Oh," Wolff said, leaning over her plate. "Sorry Legs,

37

I didn't mean to keep you from your . . . noodles and . . . Just what is that stuff anyway?"

"Beef stroganoff," she said.

"I didn't know cows did that," Mugabe said with a straight face.

Gunner exploded with laughter.

"Looks good," Wolff said, smacking his lips. "I think I'll have some. It'll save me a little time later."

Both Gunner and Mugabe howled.

"Why don't you two clowns give it a rest," Sandra said tiredly, laying her napkin on the table and pushing her chair back. "You should have stayed in Mexico. Things were real quiet around here with you two gone."

"Well, I'm glad to see you too, Sweetheart," Wolff said, blowing her an exaggerated kiss. "How 'bout buying me a drink after dinner?"

"I, got better things to spend my money on," Sandra said, getting to her feet and walking away.

"That woman's got to learn to lighten up," Mugabe said, shaking his head as he watched her leave. "She takes life much too seriously."

"That's what comes from eating too much strokin' off," Wolff grinned.

All three men collapsed with laughter.

Chapter 6

Western Region TPF Headquarters

Later that afternoon, the Dragon Flight chopper cops assembled in the large briefing room to hear what their commander had in store for them.

"You guys got any idea what this is all about?" Gunner asked Wolff and Mugabe as he slid into a chair.

Wolff shrugged. "Beats the shit outa me, but Buzz said something about orders from Washington."

"Rumor control has it that we're going on vacation to the sunny south," one of the other pilots broke in.

"Good time of year for it," Mugabe said casually, looking out the windows at the cold November rain falling in sheets outside.

"Does rumor control say exactly what part of the sunny south we're going to be visiting?" Gunner asked.

"All I know is that charts of the Gulf Coast areas of Texas and Louisiana were requisitioned."

"Oh boy," Mugabe said, rubbing his hands together. "Cajun food, here I come."

Captain Corcran walked in right at that moment and the officers fell quiet as he strode to the podium in the front of the room.

"Okay, people," Buzz said, turning to face his officers. "Listen up. I'm sure that most of you have heard all about the latest exploits of our two ace flyers, Wolfman and Mojo, down in Mexico. If you haven't, all you missed was that they failed to keep terrorists from blowing up an American owned oil platform in the Gulf of California."

That got quite a few laughs as Wolff hid his face behind his hands.

"Anyway," Buzz continued. "This was apparently the first incident in what is being advertised as a new wave of Arab terrorism, this time aimed at American oil companies. Washington is taking this threat very seriously and we have been alerted to move Dragon Flight to the Southern Region. Our mission will be to help them guard the oil rigs in the Gulf of Mexico against any more of this kind of thing. I don't have any idea how long this operation will take, but until something breaks on this case, we'll all be whistling Dixie. We will be going with a full thirty day stockage level on all supplies and equipment."

That got everyone's attention. Buzz didn't like to move supplies unless it was absolutely necessary.

He thumbed through the thick folder. "Here's the assignments. The Griffins will take off at first light tomorrow and will fly to Bolen Air Base, Texas, an Air Force Reserve base on the Gulf coast, where we will establish our forward operating base. As Dragon Lead, officers Wolff and Mugabe will navigate. Officers Jennings and Revell will back them up and make sure they don't get lost."

That got a few chuckles.

"Since Officer Browning is still in the hospital, Simpson will remain here and ready a new Dragon One Three to replace the one they left in Mexico. As soon as that chopper is ready, it will join us.

"Lastly, Lieutenant Zumwald and his Tac Platoon will move out with the support elements later that morning. Since the C-17s are twice as fast as the Griffins, they will arrive at our destination before the choppers. Therefore, once they touch down, all I want to see is assholes and elbows from everyone. I expect the planes to be offloaded by late afternoon and I want to have everything fully operational first thing the next morning. Any questions?"

The groaning and mumbling got louder.

"Okay," he said, ignoring the groans. "You people get a good night's sleep. I'll see you on the flight line at zero six hundred tomorrow morning."

The briefing room cleared quickly as the officers hurried to take care of their personal affairs while they still had time. One of the biggest disadvantages about being a chopper cop is giving up any idea of maintaining a stable life style. At a moment's notice, they would have to pack up and head off across the country for an indefinite stay. This was also the biggest reason why so few of the chopper cops were married.

When Wolff and Mugabe walked out into the parking lot, the chill November rain was still falling. "Where do you want to go for dinner tonight, Wolfman?" Mugabe asked, pulling the collar of his flight jacket up around his ears.

"I don't know," Wolff shrugged. "Someplace that's warm and has good tequila."

"Didn't you get enough of that shit in Mexico?"

"You can never have too much of a good thing," Wolff said seriously. "Plus, I have to keep in shape in case we get called back down there again."

"How about the 'Red Baron'," Mugabe asked, referring to the popular pilot's hangout at the local general aviation airfield.

"That sounds about right."

Wolff opened the driver's door of his battered, blue '92 Mazda Miata roadster and slid in behind the steering wheel. It took a few tries before the twin cam, four cylinder, turboed engine fired up. He let it idle to warm up for a few seconds before throwing the gear shift into reverse and popping the clutch. The sports car squealed out of the parking lot backwards.

"Jesus man!" Mugabe said, frantically fumbling with the seat belt buckle. "Where'd you get your fucking driver's license?"

Wolff clutched, slam-shifted into first, dropped the clutch and the Miata shot forward, the turbocharger screaming like a Griffin's turbine.

"Same place you get your hats, asshole," he grinned. "The Goodwill."

Mugabe shook his head. This was going to be yet another one of those nights. Sometimes he wished that his partner was a little less enthusiastic about life. But what the hell, at least life around him wasn't boring.

The next morning, Mugabe was down on the flight line right as dawn broke over the mile high city of Denver. Mugabe made a point of being the first to suit up and get down to the flight line before every mission, regardless of what it was. This was something he had started doing back in the good old days when he had been flying for the CIA, the

41

DEA and anyone else who would give him a ride behind the weapons controls in the left seat of a chopper gunship.

The breaking day was cold, but clear for a change and the visibility was unlimited. If it stayed this way throughout their long flight to Texas, everything would be a piece of cake for a change.

Mugabe savored his moments alone at dawn with the hulking, silent flying machines. It was his form of meditation, to stand and drink in the silence, knowing that it would soon be gone. Before long, the flight line would be full of the chatter of air crew cursing the cold, the clanging of steel on steel as the weapons were loaded, and the whine of the starter motors as the chopper turbines were fired up.

If the truth were told, he would have preferred it to be a little warmer, more like the mountains of Colombia rather than the Rockies, but he snuggled into the fur collar of his flight jacket and watched the sun light up the distant skyline of Denver.

As the other crews started filtering in one at a time, Mugabe looked across the wet tarmac and saw Wolff heading for the flight line at a brisk walk. Surprised, he glanced down at his watch. For a change, the Wolfman was on time and he was completely dressed, the collar of his leather jacket pulled up tightly around his neck.

"We ready to go?" Wolff greeted him gruffly.

"Almost," Mugabe replied. "Red's guys are still fucking around with one of the long range tanks on One Four. They can't get it to cross feed right."

For the long flight to Texas, the three Griffins had been fitted with long range fuel tanks on the inboard hard points under the stub wings. With the 250 gallon tanks in place, the choppers could cruise some 900 miles without refueling. And, at their normal cruising speed of 175 miles an hour, that was about the limit of the crew's bladders. As hi-tech as they were, the Griffins weren't equipped with relief tubes.

"Come on, Red," Wolff muttered, stomping his feet to try to get the circulation going. "Let's get this fucking fly-

42

ing circus in the air. It's cold enough to freeze the brass nuts off a steel bridge out here."

"If I remember right, *amigo*," Mugabe reminded him. "You were the one who was in such a big fucking hurry to get back here to Denver."

"But," Wolff shot back. "I didn't say that I wanted to stand around freezing my balls off on the flight line, did I? What I had in mind was lying in front of the fireplace in my apartment teaching some sweet young thing the finer points of life."

"Who'd you have in mind for that duty?"

Wolff shrugged. "I don't know, I haven't had time to recruit her yet."

"Why don't you try that program out on Legs?"

"She's too smart," Wolff grinned. "Also, she's all sorts of pissed off at me again."

"When are you two going to kiss and make up?"

Wolff got a funny look on his face. "Just what in the hell are you talking about, Mojo?"

Mugabe slowly shook his head. "Haven't you figured it out yet?"

"Figured out what?"

The copilot grinned broadly. "Man, for a guy who's supposed to be as smart as you are, you can sure be a dumb shit sometimes."

"What in the fuck are you talking about, man?"

"You and Legs," Mugabe replied. "When are you two going to quit acting like grade school kids and get down to business."

Red's arrival kept Wolff from answering, "You're ready to go now, Wolfman," the maintenance chief said.

" 'Bout fucking time," the pilot snapped. "I'm freezing my nuts off out here."

"At least you still have some to freeze off," Red said. "You lose any of these ships this time and you're going to be singing soprano in the Dallas boys choir."

Wolff shook his head as he climbed into the right seat of his ship and buckled himself in. It was too damned cold to

43

have to listen to Red's ritual of bitching and biting today. He plugged in his helmet cord and keyed his mike.

"This is Dragon Lead," he radioed to the other two ships. "Let's fire 'em up and get the hell outa here."

The other two pilots were just as anxious as he was to get airborne and turn the cockpit heaters on and they answered him immediately. In seconds, the high-pitched whine of starter motors and the smell of burning kerosene filled the chill air as the three Griffins came alive. The pounding beat of their rotors echoed from the hangar building as the turbines spooled up faster and faster.

"Dragon Flight, this is Lead, send status."

As soon as the other pilots called in that they were go, Wolff keyed his mike again and called the Tactical Operations Center. "Dragon Control," he radioed, "This is Dragon Lead, we are ready for takeoff."

"Dragon Control, copy," came Mom's voice. "You are clear to go. Good Luck."

"Dragon Flight, this is Lead," Wolff radioed as he nudged forward on the cyclic control and pulled pitch to the rotor blades. "Let's get this show on the road."

In a low ground effect hover, Wolff taxied One Zero out onto the end of the runway with the other two Griffins close behind. The pilot twisted the throttle and hauled up on the collective, making the sharklike ship leap up into the clear, cold sky. With One Zero leading, the two Griffins formed into a vee and circled the airbase before turning south like geese heading down to Mexico for the winter.

"Where's our mid-point stop?" Mugabe asked, settling back for a little nap.

"Oklahoma City," Wolff said.

"Good. Just in time for lunch."

Chapter 7

Bolen Air Base, Texas

Cut into the mesquite thickets of the Texas coastal plain south of Houston, Bolen Field, as it had been known back in the 1940s, had once echoed to the throbbing roar of Pratt and Whitney R-1830 piston engines pulling B-24 Liberators into the sky. A bomber crew training base in World War II, Bolen Field had been renamed in the fifties and became a Texas Air National Guard training base, playing host to a squadron of screaming F-86 Saber jets. With the cutback in military forces in the early '90s, Bolen had hung on as an Air Force Reserve training station that was primarily used as a staging point for aircraft flying the drug interdiction missions over the Gulf of Mexico.

Over the last few years, the Air Force station support personnel had grown accustomed to taking care of the TPF Griffins and their flight crews. As soon as the three machines of Dragon Flight appeared over the runway, the ground crew assembled to care for them after the long flight from Denver. When the choppers taxied in front of the hangar and shut down their rotors, a gang of airmen swarmed over them, refueling and checking them out.

"I like the service around here," Mugabe commented, watching the blue Air Force fuel truck pull up alongside their ship. "A real first class act. It makes me feel like someone special, a VIP."

"Just wait 'till Red shows his ugly face," Wolff laughed. "He'll take care of that feeling real quick. Five minutes with him chewing your ass about something and you'll think you're a fucking rookie again."

A man in a blue TPF uniform with sergeant stripes on his sleeves emerged from the operations building and hurried over to the two flyers. "Who's the flight leader here?" he asked abruptly.

"I am," Wolff said, sticking his hand out. "Sergeant Rick Wolff, Dragon One Zero. This is my copilot, Jumal Mugabe."

"How soon can you get these birds back up in the air?" the sergeant asked anxiously, skipping the polite introductions completely.

"That depends on who you are," Wolff said, staring the shorter man down. "And exactly what it is that you want us to do."

"I'm sorry," the man said, sticking out his hand. "I'm Jim Boston, the flight ops sergeant around here. We just had one of our ships go down for major work and I need to use one of your Griffins to fill the gap till we can get it back on line."

"Well, we've just flown twelve hundred miles and we're a little beat," Wolff replied. "Do you have something positive for us to check out, or do you just want us to cruise up and down the coast looking for bad guys?"

"We just need you to cover one of our patrol areas," the sergeant went on to explain. "But if I don't get someone up there ASAP, my ass is going to be in a real crack. I cleared it with your operations people and they told me to talk to you about it."

Wolff sighed. "Okay, I'll take it myself. Let me take a leak first and get a quick cup of coffee."

"I'll go see if I can round up some of Zoomie's boys to go with us," Mugabe said.

"Yeah, while you're at it, tell Gunner that he's on ramp alert tonight."

"He'll love that."

"Fuck him if he can't take a joke," Wolff grinned wickedly. "And you can tell him that I said that."

"Okay," Wolff turned back to the flight ops sergeant. "Where can I find that coffee?"

A few minutes later, Wolff was standing by the open door of his ship finishing off his coffee and looking over the map of his patrol area when Lieutenant Jack Zumwald caught up with him. "Mojo said that you need a Tac Team?" the Tactical Platoon leader asked.

"That's right, Zoomie, I've got to go out on patrol and need some people in the back."

"No sweat," Zumwald replied. "I'll round up some of the boys and go with you myself. If I hang around here, Red will just put me to work setting up the TOC."

Zumwald turned around and spotted some of his Tac Platoon people working to offload the equipment that had come in on the last C-17 from Denver. He let out a piercing whistle and one of the men looked up. Zumwald made a circling motion over his head and then, making a clenched fist, pumped his arm up and down twice.

Five men detached themselves from the work party and double timed over to their platoon leader.

"Grab your gear and hop in One Zero," Zumwald said. "We're going for a ride."

The Tac Team ran for their weapons and equipment. They were back in less than two minutes, pulling on their gear as they scrambled into the back of Wolff's Griffin.

For these patrol missions, Zumwald's Tac Platoon had been broken down into four, five man Tactical Teams, one for each Griffin. And, since they had no idea what kind of tactical situation they might encounter, they were carrying a mixed weapons load. Three of the men in each team were armed with the H and K MP-5 9mm submachineguns, one man carried a Styer SSG 7.62mm sniper's rifle and the fifth packed a 12 gauge Franchi automatic shotgun/grenade launcher.

Backing up the long arms, each man carried a Glock 10mm semi-automatic pistol, the standard man-stopping sidearm of the Tac Force. If things got so serious that they had to resort to using pistols, they wanted first round kills and the powerful 10mm round would stop a grizzly bear in his tracks and knock him over on his back. No matter what tactical situation they encountered, their weapons mix would let them take care of it with no problems.

The Tac cops were dressed in their woodland pattern camouflage SWAT uniforms, a leaf shaped pattern of brown, tan and two shades of green. Over that, they wore Kevlar body armor jackets with ceramic inserts covering their vital areas. The flak jackets were covered with the same camouflage material as their uniforms and had pouches to hold their spare magazines and tactical equipment.

Since there was a chance that they might have to deploy on the ground, they were not wearing the full set of Kevlar and ceramic armor inserts in the jackets and uniforms. Wearing the full armor inserts made them almost invulnerable to small arms fire, but also dramatically restricted their mobility.

Camouflaged Kevlar helmets with full lexan face shields and nose filters completed their combat uniforms. The helmets contained voice activated commo gear and earphone plugs that allowed the team members to communicate with each other even over the roar of gunfire. The helmet radios could also be used switched over to talk to the Griffins and the Tactical Operations Center.

While Wolff and Mugabe completed their preflight checks, Zumwald climbed into the back of Wolff's Griffin, stowed his MP-5 and plugged his helmet radio cord into the chopper's intercom plug so he could talk to the crew. "We're ready back here, Wolfman," he called up to the pilot.

"Ya'll just sit back and make your little selves comfortable, you hear?" Mugabe answered in his best southern drawl as Wolff cracked the throttle open to flight idle and pulled the starting trigger. The still warm turbines started with a whine that quickly rose to a shriek. As soon as the main rotor blades came up to speed, Wolff gently hauled up on the collective, lifting the Griffin off the helipad in a low ground effect hover. He nudged down on the rudder pedal, swinging her tail around to line up with the runway.

He paused in a hover long enough to click in his throat

mike. "Dragon Control, this is Dragon One Zero. We're ready to roll."

"One Zero," came Mom's familiar voice. "This is Dragon Control. You are clear for takeoff. Vector zero nine zero after takeoff."

"One Zero, copy."

Twisting the throttle all the way up against the stop, Wolff pushed forward on the cyclic control. The chopper's tail rose and she started down the runway in a classic gunship takeoff. As soon as his airspeed came up, the pilot hauled up on the collective, pulling pitch on the rotor blades. The blades bit deeper into the air and the sleek, dark blue machine leapt up into the south Texas sky.

Climbing to a low cruising altitude, Wolff flew out to the coast and turned south. In the rear compartment, Zumwald's men settled in for the long flight. Out came the paperbacks and the deck of cards. Sometimes waiting for something to happen was far worse than being right in the middle of a hot firefight. But at least while they were airborne, they wouldn't have Red yelling at them.

Zumwald, however, was not bored. He was never bored when there was even the faintest possibility of action. Action was the reason why Zoomie had joined the Tac Force in the first place. Mountain climbing, skydiving and static jumping just hadn't been exciting enough for him. He had craved bigger and better adrenaline highs and that was exactly what commanding the Tac Platoon had given him. Even on a routine patrol mission like today, where he faced long hours in the back of a Griffin with no promise of a firefight at the end of the ride, there was still the possibility that the Tac Team would go into action and that was enough for him.

He looked out the window at the mesquite covered coastal plains passing by below them. From five thousand feet, Texas looked calm and serene. He just hoped that it all wasn't going to be that peaceful. That would be boring and Zoomie Zumwald hated to be bored.

* * *

49

"Dragon One Zero, this is Dragon Control," came Mom's raspy voice over Wolff's headphones.

"One Zero, go ahead," Wolff answered.

"This is Control. We have just received an emergency call from a refinery in your patrol area. They say that they are under attack by terrorists who flew in by helicopter."

"One Zero, copy," Wolff answered. "What's their location?"

"It's the Texaco refinery at Beaumont."

"Good copy," Wolff radioed as he punched the location into his navigational computer. "We are Code Twenty to that location, ETA sixteen minutes."

"Control copy. We are scrambling Dragon One Four and vectoring him into that location for your backup. His ETA is thirty-five minutes. Be advised Rules of Engagement Bravo are in effect."

"One Zero, copy," Wolff grinned. ROE Bravo meant that they could shoot back at anyone who shot at them without having to clear it with the TOC first. It was open season on bad guys in Texas.

Banking the Griffin over to the new heading, Wolff twisted the throttle all the way against the stop, hit the overrev switch on the turbine governors and flattened the pitch on the rotor blades for maximum speed. At 110 percent RPM, most of the ship's forward thrust was provided by the exhausts of the howling GE T-700 turbines and the stub wings provided most of the lift as the ship's speed built. At almost 275 miles an hour, they'd be on the scene in minutes.

Wolff clicked in on the intercom. "Zoomie," the pilot said. "This is the Wolfman. Better wake your boys up back there. We've got work to do."

"What's up?" Zumwald called back.

"Not sure. Mom says that they have a report of armed terrorists attacking a refinery so you'd better have your guys lock and load."

"What's our ETA?"

"We'll be there in about fourteen minutes."

"We'll be ready."

Behind his face shield, Wolff felt his face break out in a big grin as the adrenaline started racing through his body. He loved the blood-singing, gut-tightening feeling that came every time he went into action. He tightened his gloved fingers around the cyclic and collective controls, delicately coaxing every last mile an hour he could get out of his howling turbines. The sooner he got there, the better. Like Zoomie, Wolff hated to be bored.

Wolff and Mugabe saw the tall column of billowing, greasy black smoke staining the clear Texas sky on the outskirts of Beaumont long before they could see the burning refinery. Whatever was going on down there, they were too late to prevent it. All they could do now was try to get the guys who had done this.

"Zoomie!" Wolff called back. "We have an incident down there, the whole place is burning."

"Copy," Zumwald answered curtly as he fixed the strap of his H and K under the epaulet of his flak vest. His men had also secured their weapons and were ready to unass the chopper as soon as Wolff touched down. It was not going to be a boring day after all.

"There's the chopper!" Mugabe said pointing to the dark green camouflage painted Aerospatiale SA. 390 Super Puma sitting on the ground outside the fence surrounding the refinery compound. Its five bladed rotor was turning over at an idle and the side doors to the passenger compartment were slid open.

"I've got him," Wolff grinned, kicking the Griffin's tail around to line up on the other chopper. "Let's see what he does when I buzz him."

As the nose of the Griffin dropped into a screaming dive, Wolff saw the figures of eight men in camouflage uniforms and carrying weapons break from the main gate of the burning refinery and race for the grounded chopper. "Talk to 'em, Mojo," he said.

The gunner flicked the switch to the external loudspeaker system and clicked in his throat mike. "On the ground, this is the United States Tactical Police. Drop your weapons and stop where you are or we will . . ."

The last of the eight men racing for the chopper whirled around. Raising his assault rifle to his shoulder, he ripped off a long burst at the diving Griffin. That was just what Wolff had wanted him to do. Now they could shoot back without any further formalities.

Instinctively, Wolff slammed the cyclic over to the upper right side, stomped down on the right rudder pedal and pulled course pitch to the rotor blades. The speeding Griffin shuddered as the sudden torque increase threw the ship into a hard banked, skidding right turn. The stream of fire from the ground found only empty air where the Griffin had been just an instant before.

Snapping the tail even farther around to the right, Wolff dumped his pitch. The chopper flipped over onto her left side and fell like a stone. The pilot kicked down on the right rudder pedal and slammed the cyclic stick into the upper right corner, suddenly leveling out and snapping the Griffin's tail around to aim her nose at the terrorists' chopper.

"Control, this is One Zero X-Ray," Mugabe radioed. "We are under fire from armed terrorists."

"Dragon Control, copy. Don't let them get away."

"One Zero, copy."

Chapter 8

Beaumont, Texas

In the left seat, Mugabe had already armed his turret weapons and had selected the ammunition he wanted to use on this target. The 25mm Chain Gun was switched over to an armor-piercing and tracer round mix and the 40mm grenade launcher was feeding straight HE loads. Mojo was ready to rock and roll.

"Take 'em out, Mojo!" Wolff shouted.

The black gunner centered the grounded Super Puma in the HUD sight on his helmet visor and tightened his gloved fingers around the firing controls, his right hand on the trigger to the Chain Gun and the left hand on the 40mm button. As soon as the red glowing numbers on the digital readout told him that he was in range, he triggered the Chain Gun.

The Griffin shuddered as Mugabe opened up. A stream of red tracer fire raced down to connect with the Super Puma's engine compartment. Not only was the Chain Gun fast, it was accurate. The turret's gun aiming system automatically compensated for recoil, re-aiming the gun ten times a second while it was firing. As long as Mugbe had the target locked in his gunsight, he would hit it. And hit it he did.

The 25mm armor-piercing and tracer rounds tore into the terrorist's chopper. The armor-piercing rounds shattered the spinning turbine compressor blades. The jagged broken steel blades cut through the pressurized fuel feed lines. JP-4 jet fuel sprayed into the air and the tracer rounds exploded the spraying fuel.

A ball of fire engulfed the top of the chopper, halting the running men in their tracks and sending them on their faces in the dirt. There was no way they would fly away to safety now. Getting to their feet, they dashed for cover in the woodline fifty meters away.

"Zoomie!" Wolff called back. "They're taking to the woods!"

"I see 'em," the Tac Platoon leader called back. "Get us on the ground!"

"Landing now!"

As Wolff bored in closer to the target, Mugabe shifted his fire back toward the chopper's tail boom. Although Rules of Engagement Bravo allowed him to shoot to kill, he wanted to finish taking out the chopper without killing all of the crew. They needed someone left alive to interrogate later.

As Mugabe watched the two terrorist air crew struggling to get out of the cockpit of their doomed machine, a boiling angry red and black fireball suddenly exploded engulfing the ship. The flames had reached the chopper's JP-4 fuel tanks.

"Ah shit!" Mugabe muttered.

Keeping the nose of the Griffin lined up with the blazing wreckage of the burning Super Puma, Wolff flared out and came in for a hot landing. No sooner had the Griffin's skids touched the ground before the side doors slid open and Zumwald's Tac Team came pouring out of the back and raced after the terrorists.

The Tac Cops hadn't run more than ten meters, however, before a burst of automatic fire from the woodline sent them flat on their faces. This was not going to be as easy as it looked. Whoever these guys were, they sure as hell knew what they were doing.

Mugabe had been ready for something like that, however. With a twitch of his wrist, he swung the nose turret over and sent a long burst of return fire into the woodline. The HE rounds chewed up the brush and the terrorist fire cut off abruptly. Wolff quickly pulled pitch and the Griffin leaped back up into the air.

"Zoomie, this is the Wolfman," the pilot radioed. "We'll fly cover for you."

"Roger," the Tac Platoon leader snapped, his face pressed in the dirt. "Get on it!"

Wolff was over the woodline in a split second, but the brush was too thick for Mugabe to find his targets optically. He flipped over to radar tracking and shook his head again. He had lost them.

"Tac One," Wolff radioed, "There's a swamp right beyond the woodline. I think they were in there."

"Tac One, copy. We're on the way now."

Lieutenant Zumwald took the point position himself as the five man Tac Team moved out again. With the Griffin hovering protectively overhead, they quickly pushed on through the scrub brush and cactus to reach the edge of the swamp. Other than a few scuffed boot prints leading down into the water and a little silt rising from the disturbed bottom mud, there was no sign of their suspects.

"One Zero, this is Tac One," Zumwald called up to the Griffin. "It looks like they took to the swamp, probably moving to the north."

"One Zero, good copy. Be advised that the map shows that swamp extends a good ten miles or so and it's a couple of miles wide."

"Shit!" Zumwald muttered. This was going to be a real bitch.

With the Griffin hovering protectively overhead, Zumwald used hand and arm signals to order his team to spread out behind him and he called the sniper into the slack position right behind him to back him up with the scoped weapon as he stepped out into the swamp. The brackish water was warm, but the mud clung to his boots making every step an effort.

Zoomie was painfully aware that even with the air cover, he and his men were sitting ducks for anyone lying in ambush. He carefully scanned the water and bank ahead of him for any signs of the terrorists, silt kicked up, anything, but he saw nothing out of the ordinary.

A few minutes later, the Tac Team leader noticed that the shadows were lengthening and glanced down at his watch. In the half hour that had passed since Wolff had first spotted the plume of oil smoke in the sky, the sun had fallen behind the stumpy mesquite trees, leaving the swamp in shadow. In another half hour, it would be completely dark. If they were going to catch up with these guys, they needed help.

"One Zero, this is Tac One," Zumwald radioed. "I'm going to need some help with this or these guys are going to get away from me in the dark."

"One Zero, copy," Wolff answered. "Gunner's on the way with another one of your Tac Teams in the back. Where do you want me to put them down?"

Zumwald stopped long enough to consult his map. "There's a spit of land two clicks north of here that juts out into the swamp. Have him drop them there in a blocking position facing south."

"One Zero, good copy." Wolff answered. "They'll be on the ground in ten minutes."

Zumwald slapped at a mosquito as he put the map away. "Move out," he whispered into the microphone of his helmet radio.

Ten minutes later, the voice of Gunner Jennings in Dragon One Four broke into Zumwald's helmet ear phones. "Tac One, this is One four," the pilot radioed.

"Tac One, go," Zumwald answered, speaking softly.

"This is One Four. Be advised that Tac Two is on the ground at nine-seven-four, two-eight-three."

"Tac One, good copy. I'll work them from here. Thanks."

Zumwald flicked the radio over to the platoon frequency. "Tac Two, this is Tac One."

"Tac Two, go," came the voice of Sergeant Garcia, Tac Two's team leader.

"Tac One. I want you to spread your people out along the southern side of that spit of land. We're chasing at least eight men and they are well armed. Have your sniper switch over to night vision mode and keep him busy with that scope. Everyone stay on your toes, these guys we're looking for are real pros. How copy."

"Tac Two, good copy."

By this time, it was completely dark in the swamp. Zumwald snapped his night vision goggles down over his eyes and moved out again. Even with the goggles, the swamp was an impenetrable patchwork of shadows and vague shapes. Out in the open the way they were, if the terrorists had any kind of night vision gear, there was no way he would be able to see them before they saw him. It was time to put the Griffins to work.

"One Zero, this is Tac One."

"One Zero, go ahead."

"I can't see shit down here, Wolfman, can you light things up for us?"

"Copy, Nightsun coming up now. Watch your eyes."

The swamp suddenly became bright as day as the twin beams of the SX-18 Nightsun spotlights in the belly of the hovering Griffin flicked on. Wolff switched them over to wide beam and maneuvered his ship higher in the sky to give them the greatest possible coverage.

"How's that?" he radioed to the man on the ground.

"Tac One. Just fine, Wolfman. Just keep the beams well ahead of us. I don't want them lighting us up as well."

"Good copy."

With the lights on wide beam, the swamp now took on the aspect of a huge stage. The interplay of brightly lit areas flanked by deep shadow made it even more difficult for Zumwald to see clearly. The light had also awakened the swamp dwellers who had turned in for the night, filling the air with the chatter of birds and the calls of reptiles.

Zumwald was just about to ask Wolff to turn the lights off when, from two hundred meters in front of him, the chatter of an assault rifle on automatic fire cut off all the other sounds. A stream of tracer fire reached up into the night sky and slammed into the belly of Wolff's Griffin, shattering one of the Nightsun lights. Zumwald's team dove for cover in the trees along the bank.

As Wolff zoomed up into the air to get out of the line of fire, Mugabe triggered a quick burst to cover their retreat and the pilot switched off the remaining light. Maybe using spotlights on these guys wasn't such a bright idea after all.

"Did you get a make on that position?" Wolff called down to Zumwald.

"I think so," he answered. "I'll see if I can put some tracer fire on it for you."

Zumwald slid a magazine of tracer ammunition into the well of his MP-5 and sighted in on where he thought the terrorist fire had come from. He triggered off three quick shots and ducked back down into cover. The only problem with using tracer fire at night was that while they helped you see where your rounds were hitting, they also showed the enemy the position you were firing from.

Zoomie's instincts were right on. No sooner had he ducked back down than a burst of fire shredded the foliage right above his head.

"I've got him," Wolff radioed. "Stand by while we try to dust his ass."

The noise of the Griffin's rotors grew louder as Wolff dove down from a dark night sky. With all the navigation and cockpit lights turned off, the dead black skin of the chopper could not be seen. The roar of the Chain Gun broke the stillness, punctuated by the deep cough of the 40mm grenade launcher.

The swamp was lit with the flashes of the exploding shells as Mugabe walked his fire through an area as big as a football field.

As abruptly as it had started, the Griffin's fire cut off. "Tac One, this is One Zero," Wolff radioed. "See if that did anything to discourage them."

"Copy. We're moving out now."

Zumwald slid the night vision goggles down over his eyes. "Okay boys," he called to his team over his helmet radio. "Let's move out."

The Tac Team slipped noiselessly back into the swamp and headed for the tangled copse that Mugabe had dusted. Zumwald felt absolutely naked as they moved out into the open. One man with a night scope could put all of them in the bag in seconds. He felt sweat break out as he swept his eyes from side, trying to pierce the darkness.

In what seemed like an eternity later, he reached the first sign of the explosive rounds the Griffin had fired. Ordering his men to fan out on either side of him, they carefully searched the area. Nothing. Whoever had been there had beat feet before the chopper had opened up.

"One Zero," he radioed up to Wolff. "This is Tac One, no one's home."

"Try a little farther to your left," the pilot radioed back. "Mojo's having a little trouble with his sensors working in the swamp, but he thinks that he picked up some movement over there.''

"Copy," Zumwald called back. "We're moving out now."

Zumwald looked over in the direction that Wolff had indicated, but all he could see was a dark mass reaching up several meters in the sky. It was probably a tangled clump of cypress trees, an ideal spot for an ambush.

"Move out," he ordered.

Chapter 9

Deep in the swamp

Zumwald's team spread out on line as they headed for the objective. The going was slow as the men tried to negotiate the treacherous swamp bottom without stepping in a hole and going in over their heads. About a quarter of the way there, a shot rang out, sending the men scrambling for what little cover there was available.

"We've got it," Wolff radioed before Zumwald could even hit the switch on his own radio. "Watch your heads."

The beat of the chopper's rotors drowned out all the other swamp sounds as Wolff made a quick firing run with the Chain Gun. While covered by the chopper's gunfire, Zumwald and his men raced for cover back where they had started from. As soon as they got in place, they added fire from their weapons.

"One Zero, Tac One," Zumwald called once he was safely behind the trunk of a huge cypress.

"One Zero, go."

"Tac One, I'm going to try to maneuver Tac Two into position to cover the other side of that position."

"I don't recommend doing that, Zoomie," Wolf radioed back. "Mojo's having a lot of trouble picking up movement down there. There's too much background clutter for the sensors to penetrate. I'm afraid that we might take them for our bad guys and shoot them up by mistake."

"Tac One, you're right," Zumwald answered.

A thousand meters over the swamp, Wolff did a figure eight orbit over the swamp while Mugabe bent over his sensor readouts. They were at a Mexican standoff right now, neither Zumwald or the terrorists could move.

"I've got movement coming out the back," Mugabe said, as he triggered off a short burst from the Chain Gun. As soon as the readout cleared after the explosions of the 25mm rounds, the movement was gone.

"I think we can keep 'em boxed in," he told Wolff.

"Good, I don't want to have to go chasing them all over Texas in the morning."

Back on the ground, Zumwald realized if he tried to move on the terrorists' position they'd get cut up in the open and if the terrorists tried to sneak away, the Griffin would spot them and shoot them up. He settled down for a long wait.

There was one option that Zumwald hadn't considered: the terrorists trying to overrun his position by stealth or frontal assault. A few minutes later, when Wolff's chopper was on the outbound leg of his orbit, the terrorists opened up on Zumwald's position with a blistering hail of automatic weapons fire.

The Tac Team tried to return fire without exposing themselves, but all they could do was to keep their heads down. Wolff was back on site in mere seconds, but by that time, the enemy fire cut off and Mugabe couldn't find a target.

"Why the fuck did they do that?" Mugabe muttered, his eyes scanning his readouts and his fingers resting on his weapons controls.

"Diversion," Wolff said. "Check the area right in front of Zoomie's position."

Mugabe did as Wolff suggested and picked up the faint tracks of doppler movement close in to the Tac Team's position. "Tac One, One Zero X-ray" he called down. "I've got movement to your left front, maybe fifty meters. They're too close for me to fire."

"Copy."

"Sniper!" Zoomie called over the team radio. "Left front fifty meters!"

The sniper focused his scope and peered out into the darkness. The faint light of the stars amplified by his scope turned the swamp into a fantasy scene of light and dark green shadows. He thought he saw something in the water. It might have been a gator, but he fired anyway.

Immediately, the terrorists opened up again with everything they had. Obviously, the sniper had spotted someone trying to close in on them. Mugabe started in on the Chain Gun and grenades again and the terrorists' fire faded as they dove for cover.

Zumwald saw that no more fire was coming from the terrorists' position and shouted. "Cease fire! Cease fire!"

For a few seconds, silence reigned over the swamp. Then ever so slowly, the local inhabitants took up their cries again now that the humans had stopped making such a racket and they could hear themselves.

"Tac One, this is the Wolfman. They've gone to ground again," the pilot reported. "Mojo can't pick them up anymore. What do you want me to do now?"

"We've just got to sit and wait 'em out," Zoomie answered. "How long can you stay on station?"

"I've got another ten minutes or so before I'm bingo fuel, but I can get One Four back up into the air to keep an eye on them while I go back to top off."

"You'd better do that. Even with the Starlights, I can't see shit in here and if they start moving again, I need you to spot for me."

"One Zero, good copy," Wolff answered. "Gunner will contact you in just a minute."

The silence was unnerving as the sound of Wolff's chopper faded into the distance. It was comforting to have the beat of her powerful rotors overhead. In a few moments, however, Gunner's voice broke into Zumwald's head-phones. "Tac One, this is One four. We're airborne and will be on station in zero two."

"Tac One, copy." It was nice to know that Legs would soon be upstairs with her hands on the triggers.

The rest of the long night passed slowly, but uneventfully. There was no activity from the terrorists. When it was his turn to stand down from watch, Zumwald found that it was impossible to get much rest. When it wasn't the mosquitos making strafing runs on every inch of his exposed skin, it was a stick poking him in the leg or a bug crawling up the back of his neck. All told, he was one miserable Tactical Platoon leader.

For the rest of the night, the Griffins traded off keeping station above Zumwald's Tac Team, their sensor battery on full blast looking for any sign of the terrorists. But there was nothing, no IR traces, no doppler readout, no audio pickup, no nothing.

It was deathly quiet in the little Texas swamp.

A thin winter sun broke over the swamp. Even though they were just a few miles from the Gulf of Mexico, the morning was damp and chill and wisps of fog drifted in and out of the cypress trees and tangled brush. It looked like a scene straight out of a photograph in the National Geographic magazine, but Zumwald was in no mood to sit in the mud and enjoy it. He was cold, wet and miserable. All he wanted to do was to get this over with as soon as he could and go take a hot shower. But first, there was a little matter of eight armed terrorists to be taken care of.

There had been no sign of movement from them for the last several hours and there was no way to tell if they were still in the area or had managed to slip away unseen during the night. He knew that he could screw around looking for them for the rest of the day and, while playing guerrilla had been fun for a while, he knew that his men were as cold and as wet as he was and he wanted to get them out of the swamp. He thought that a massive show of force might convince the terrorists to hang it up as a lost cause.

"One Zero," he radioed. "This is Tac one. Come in."

"This is One Zero," Wolff answered. "Good morning, Zoomie. What's up?"

"This is Tac One, how about calling up another Griffin and blowing the shit out of this swamp? Maybe we can convince these maggots to give up."

"This is One Zero, Gunner's due to show up here in just a few minutes and we can put on a Mad Minute for you."

"What's a Mad Minute?"

Wolff laughed. "Just wait, you'll love it."

A few minutes later, Zoomie heard the beating rotors of the second chopper. "Okay," Wolff radioed. "Where do you want your little firepower demonstration?"

"This is Tac One. Put it off to the side of where you were firing last night, I want to get as many of these guys alive as I can."

"This is One Zero, wait one."

"Tac One," Wolff came back. "This is One Zero. One Mad Minute on the way."

Suddenly, the air was rent with the roar of two Griffin Chain Guns firing at once, the 1800 rounds a minute of 25mm HE rounds shredded the jungle. The Chain Gun's fire was immediately joined by the barking cough of two slower firing 40mm grenade launchers spraying HE grenades. It sounded like the end of the world had come to Texas. Now Zumwald knew why Wolff had called it a Mad Minute. A little of that could drive a man mad.

As suddenly as it had began, it stopped and silence fell over the swamp. Even the birds were quiet. As soon as the last echo of the crashing guns and exploding grenades faded away, Zumwald keyed the mike to his helmet radio. The transmission was routed through the loudspeaker system in the Griffins hovering over head.

"This is Lieutenant Zumwald of the United States Federal Tactical Police. Lay down your weapons and come out with your hands in the air. I have another unit moving in behind you and there is no way that you can escape. Give up now and save yourselves a lot of trouble."

"Okay, Mate," came a voice from behind a large tree not fifty meters to his front. "Cease fire! I'm coming out."

Zumwald was shocked when he realized just how close they had been able to get to his position during the night. Had they wanted to, they could have attacked and the Griffins wouldn't have been able to fire on them for fear of hitting the friendlies.

"Make sure you keep your hands up where I can see them," Zumwald warned.

A slender man stepped out from behind the cypress tree with his empty hands held high above his head. His splinter pattern camouflage uniform was wet and muddy and he wore a battered, faded maroon beret with a silver badge on the front, the headgear of the famous British Parachute Regiment, the Paras. Zumwald caught a brief glimpse of the man standing behind him. He was wearing the light blue beret of the British SAS, the Special Air Service, their Special Forces.

Suddenly Zumwald realized who they were dealing with here. These weren't run of the mill Arab terrorist crazies, these men were mercenaries, professional soldiers, and they were more than likely Brits or Australians.

Just what in the hell was going on here?

The mercenary came to a halt three paces in front of Zumwald and executed a snappy British Army style open handed salute. "Staff Sergeant George Ames, late of the Parachute Regiment."

"I'm Lieutenant Jack Zumwald, United States Tactical Police Force," Zoomie answered, ignoring the man's salute. "Tell your men to surrender and to come on out with their hands over their heads."

"One of me mates stopped one back there, Leftenant," the mercenary leader said, dropping his salute. "And he can't walk. I'd like to bring him out so he can be treated."

"Only if all of your people surrender now."

Sergeant Ames looked around at the men of the Tac Team

and seemed to consider the odds. "Looks like you have us by the short and curlies, Leftenant," he said with a slight shrug. "We'll call it a day."

"Tell your men to be real careful," Zumwald said. "And to come out with their weapons at sling arms. If they make any sudden movements, we'll open fire."

"Not to worry, mate," the mercenary said wearily. "We've about had our fill." He glanced up at Wolff's and Jennings' hovering Griffins. "Bloody choppers," he muttered.

"Okay lads!" he called out to his men. "The Yank Leftenant says to sling arms and come out slowly with your hands high. And no mucking about now."

Slowly, the remaining mercenaries appeared, their assault rifles slung over their shoulders, muzzles down, and their hands held high over their heads. One of them with a muddy, blood-soaked bandage tied around his thigh was supported by another man.

"I only count seven men," Zumwald said. "Where's the other one?"

"Nigel," Ames said softly. "Poor bloody bastard, he didn't make it."

Two of the Tac cops stepped out into the open to relieve the mercs of their weapons and to secure their hands behind their backs while the others kept them covered. Zoomie's men weren't about to take any chances with these guys. They were too good.

"What's the drill now, Leftenant?" the mercenary leader asked as soon as his men were disarmed.

"You are all under arrest," Zumwald answered. "And will be taken to a federal detention center where your wounded will receive medical attention. Later you will be charged as terrorists in a federal court."

Sergeant Ames slowly shook his head. "Molly, old girl," he said softly. "You were right. I am getting too bloody old for this line of work."

"You're going to be a lot older than you are now, Mister, before you find yourself a new profession," Zumwald said, pulling his handcuffs from the back of his harness. "Put your hands behind your back."

The mercenary shrugged and turned around. A federal prison cell was better than an unmarked grave in a Texas swamp.

Chapter 10

Bolen Air Base, Texas

There was a sizeable crowd waiting at the flight line when Wolff and Mugabe touched down with the back of their Griffin loaded with prisoners. Everyone in Dragon Flight had followed the battle on the radio and wanted a look at the men who had caused the chopper cops so much trouble. All they saw though, were tired, defeated men in muddy camouflage uniforms with their hands cuffed behind their backs.

The paramedics were on hand and quickly saw to the wounded mercenaries while the rest of the men were hustled into a Black Maria and whisked away to the federal detention center for what promised to be a lengthy interrogation.

"Here they are, Captain," Wolff said when he reported to Buzz. "All ready for the boys in the field office to go to work on 'em."

"It's too bad that the two in the chopper didn't make it," Buzz remarked.

"I know," Wolff shrugged. "But we should be able to get what we need from these guys."

"I hope so."

The TPF field office in Houston was providing support services for Dragon Flight while they were away from their home base. Part of that support included local investigation and interrogation of suspects. The Tactical Police Act gave the TPF the authority to use chemical interrogation on suspects involved in terrorist acts when doing so would provide speedy information that would potentially save lives. Saving lives was the top priority in terrorist incidents and, even though no one had been killed in this latest wave yet, it was only a matter of time before lives would be lost. Putting a man through this process required getting clearance all the way from Washington and the permission was rarely given. But this time, however, enough was at stake that Buzz knew he would have no problems getting it.

"Good work," Buzz said, glancing down at his watch. "We should have some idea of what's going on here in just a little while."

Although it usually took twenty-four hours for the chemical interrogation procedure to run its course, useful information was often available by the second hour that the drugs were working on the suspect.

"Maybe we can get this thing wrapped up and get back to Denver in time for Thanksgiving," the Dragon Flight commander said.

"I was kind of hoping we could stay here for a while," Wolff grinned. "I like the weather."

"No chance," Buzz growled. "We're going home as soon as we can. If you want to lie around in the sun, you can go on vacation and pay for it yourself."

Later that afternoon, Buzz called a meeting of his operations staff. Wolff, Zumwald, and Lieutenant Ramon Avilia, the Air Ground Operations officer, filed into Buzz's office and took seats around the conference table.

"Okay, people," Buzz said. "Listen up. I've got good news and bad news on those mercenaries Zoomie and the Wolfman policed up in the swamp this morning. The good news is that the suspects are cooperating fully with the interrogators. The bad news is that they didn't know diddly squat.

"According to the field office report, our mercenaries are all South Africans and Australians, professional soldiers of fortune who claim to have been hired by a radical Arab terrorist group, this 'Vengeance of God' bunch. They say that they were recruited in Kuwait by an Arab known to them only as Falcon. They said that about fifty men assembled and were equipped at an unknown, remote jungle location somewhere, they think, in Central America. After being broken down into teams and taking explosives refresher training, they were flown from there to their attack sites. This was the first assignment for this particular team. They have no idea who their employers are or where they are based."

"But they've got to know something," Zumwald looked puzzled.

"Nope," Buzz shook his head. "The field office people said that our suspects are spilling their guts and are telling them everything they can think of. But none of it adds up to much of anything."

"I'll bet they talked," Zumwald laughed. "They're facing twenty years in a federal slam and they're hoping like hell for a little judicial clemency if they cooperate with the authorities."

"Fat chance of that," Buzz said. "Those boys are going to do hard time for that little stunt."

Wolff thought for a moment. "Does the report say how long were they in the air enroute to the target?" he asked. "And where they were going after their extraction?"

Buzz thumbed through the report. "Their leader, that so-called Sergeant Ames, says that the flight was over four hours long."

"Shit! That means they could have come from almost anywhere."

"And," Buzz continued. "He says that they weren't told where they were going after the hit."

"Somebody is doing a real good job of keeping the troops in the dark here," Zumwald commented.

"And that somebody sure as hell knows what he's doing," Buzz added.

"So what's the next move, sir?" Zumwald asked.

"Since there's evidence of foreign involvement," Buzz replied. "I'm going to turn this over to the FBI and the CIA to see what they can turn up."

"Good luck with the FBI," Zumwald laughed. "That bunch usually can't find their own asses with both hands and a strong flashlight."

"The FBI still has their place," Wolff reminded his fellow chopper cop. "We need them to find the bad guys for us so we can kick their asses."

"But they always try to take the credit for our operations," Zoomie complained.

"They can have the credit for all I care," Wolff laughed. "As long as we get the body count."

"If you people are through patting yourselves on the back," Buzz said. "Can we get along with the rest of the briefing?"

Everyone shut up.

"Now this incident at the refinery last night has put this situation in a new light. We now know that we aren't up against a bunch of wild eyed fanatics, our opponents are well armed and well trained professionals. Even so, Washington is concerned that if we have any more of this kind of shootout, someone is going to get hurt."

"That goes for me too," Zumwald added. "We were lucky that none of my people were hit last night. Those guys were playing for keeps."

"Anyway, they are putting the pressure on the Southern Region commander to get this thing under control ASAP. And, since we are working for the Southern Region now, the pressure is on us too."

"But we don't have anything to work with," Zumwald pointed out the obvious. "If we had a location for these guys, we could put them out of business."

"I know, I know," Buzz said in frustration. "All we can do for now is to keep our eyes open and try to shortstop any more of this from happening. The Southern Region people are advising all the oil companies in the area on how to increase their security and are assisting them any way they can. Maybe if they keep on their toes, they can be some of help to us for a change."

"That would be nice," Zumwald said. In his experience, too often private companies resented any advice from the Tac Force, even when it would help them.

"So, until we can get more information about these people, I am stepping up the patrol schedule."

"Sir," Wolff cut in. "With only three ships, we're pushed to the limit right now."

"Dragon One Three will be arriving tomorrow morning," Buzz announced. "Browning and Simpson still aren't fully fit to return to duty so she's got a new crew."

"Who are they?"

"I don't know, they've been loaned to us from the Northern Region," Buzz replied, handing Wolff a printed schedule. "So they should be okay. Anyway, here's the patrol schedule for the evening. Any questions?"

Wolff glanced at it. "No sir."

"Okay, then," Buzz said. "That's all for now, let's get back to work."

Since Wolff and Mugabe had spent the previous night covering the action in the swamp, they were not scheduled to go out on patrol that evening, they were on ramp alert instead. That meant that as long as they stayed close to the base and kept Mom informed of their location, they had the rest of the afternoon and evening off.

"What's the score?" Mugabe asked when Wolff came out of Buzz's office.

"We're on ramp alert," the pilot answered, glancing down at his watch. "How 'bout getting dinner now, so we can get to bed early and catch up on our sack time?"

"Suits me," Mugabe answered. "You want to try the club here?"

"Sure, I don't feel like risking ptomaine at the greasy spoon across the street."

Since the Bolen Air Base was open for reserve training on the weekends, there was a small officers' club next to the main hangar and, as federal officers, the chopper cops had been given club privileges.

The first thing the pilot saw when he walked in the door of the club was Lieutenant Arturo Cuervo standing at the bar. "Yo! Cuervo!" Wolff called out. "What in the hell are you doing here?"

The Mexican officer grinned and raised his glass. "Since we did such a good job working together last time, someone thought that I should be sent up here to serve as a liaison officer between our forces in case any more rigs in Mexican waters are hit."

"Great, maybe you can get some more time in the Griffins with us."

"That's what I was hoping."

"You had dinner yet?"

"No, I just got here and thought I'd have a little of the old family recipe to wash the dust from my throat."

"Good, I'll join you," Wolff grinned. "We're on ramp alert, though, so I can only have one."

"I'm not even getting started on that shit again," Mugabe said. "I'll have a beer."

Wolff placed their drink orders and was reaching for his billfold when Cuervo laid his Unicard down on the bar. "It's on me," he said. "I'm on an expense account."

"Great," Wolff said, slapping him on the shoulder. "In that case, you can buy my dinner too."

"We Mexicans are known as a generous people, *amigo*," Cuervo laughed. "But I don't think that our generosity will stretch quite that far."

Wolff shrugged. "It was worth a try."

"Anyway," Cuervo said. "I understand that congratulations are in order for bringing back those terrorists."

"Actually, Zoomie and his boys chased them down and we just hauled them back," Wolff said modestly.

71

"But you destroyed their helicopter so they couldn't escape."

"When Ol Mojo is on the guns, he never misses."

"What did you learn from the suspects?" the Mexican asked. "Did they tell you where they were based? Or who they were working for?"

"Actually, we didn't get shit from them," Wolff sounded disgusted. "Whoever's controlling those guys is keeping his security real tight. All we learned was that they are working for some Arab who goes by the name of Falcon and that they think they were staged out of some place down in Central America."

"That's too bad," Cuervo said, "Do you have any other leads?"

"We don't have shit, *nada,*" Wolff shook his head. "All we have is a thousand miles of coastline and hundreds of oil rigs to patrol with only three choppers."

"That's going to be tough to cover with so few choppers," Cuervo said.

"You got that shit right, *amigo,*" Wolff agreed. "But remember, we're the chopper cops and we do the impossible everyday."

Cuervo laughed.

Chapter 11

Bolen Air Base

Early the next morning, Wolff met up with Arturo Cuervo in the TOC. "You doing anything right now?"

"Not really," Cuervo shrugged. "I'm just taking a look at your operation."

"Good. Grab a cup of coffee. We'll go down to the flight line and I can introduce you to the rest of Dragon Flight."

"I already had a cup in the mess hall. So let's go."

"Great."

Outside, the first crew members that Wolff ran into were that of Dragon One Four. "Yo! Gunner! Legs!" Wolff shouted. "Over here! I want you to meet somebody!"

The two officers walked over to where Wolff and Cuervo were standing by the hangars. "This is our buddy from the Mexican expedition," Wolff said. "Lieutenant Arturo Cuervo, he's up here acting as our liaison officer with the Federales now."

Sandra's eyes slowly moved over the handsome Mexican officer in the tan flight suit. "Nice to meet you," she said, extending her hand. "I'm Sandra Revell."

Cuervo took her hand and bowed over it. "A lovely name for a lovely lady," he said softly.

Sandra blushed, but didn't pull her hand back. She quickly looked down, but it was too late, the man had seen her reaction.

Wolff was amused to see Legs' usual calm, cool exterior ruffled like this. "And this is Gunner Jennings," he continued the introductions.

"I heard about your big operation down in Baja," Gunner said, sticking his hand out.

"Yes," Cuervo laughed. "Chasing terrorists who weren't there."

"Well," Gunner grinned. "You know how it goes, sometimes you get the bear, sometimes the bear gets you and sometimes it doesn't pay to go into the woods."

"But you did well here the night before last," Cuervo said.

"We got lucky, you mean," Wolff said. "If we hadn't have taken that patrol for the southern region people, those guys would have gotten away clean. Let's go meet the crews."

"Be seeing you around, Cuervo," Gunner said.

"Me too," Legs chimed in.

"I'm certain of that," the Mexican pilot smiled.

Wolff had just completed Cuervo's introduction to all the air crews of Dragon Flight when the new Dragon One Three Griffin came in for a landing. When their turbines shut down and the rotor stopped spinning, Wolff walked over to greet the new crew as they stepped out.

"I'm Rick Wolff," he said, extending his hand. "The flight leader around here."

The two new men introduced themselves as Johnson and Vargas. "I like the weather here," Johnson, the pilot, said looking up at the blue sky. "We've been freezing our asses off back in Philadelphia."

"You won't have to worry about that here," Wolff laughed. "But I hope you brought your sunscreen."

"I packed it along with my swimming suit and beach towel," Vargas said.

"Before you head for the beach I need to take you to meet the captain."

Wolff led them over to the TOC where Buzz gave them several hours off to rest up from their long flight. He instructed Wolff to schedule their first patrol for later that evening. As Wolff turned to go, Buzz reached out and handed him the new patrol schedule. "How about posting this on your way out?"

"No sweat, boss."

When Wolff took off to meet Mugabe for their morning patrol, Cuervo flew with them as an observer and to continue his training on the Griffin's systems. The three hour patrol was completely uneventful and One Zero arrived back at the base just in time to be topped off with fuel and to go on ramp alert duty.

"You want to have lunch now?" Cuervo asked as he watched Legs walk into the officers' club.

"Go ahead," Wolff said. "I've got to check in with Buzz and go over a few things first. I'll probably catch up with you later."

* * *

By mid-afternoon, the initial report was back from the CIA and Buzz called another meeting of his principal staff officers.

"Okay," Buzz said when they had gathered in his small office again. "Here's what the spooks at Langley have to say. First off, the CIA reports that the few known remaining radical Arab groups deny being involved in this incident in any way. And, for some reason best known to the arcane art of intelligence gathering, they feel that this information is accurate for a change."

That got a laugh from the chopper cops.

"And," Buzz continued. "They haven't been able to pick up any information on this new group. No one seems to have heard of the 'Vengeance of God'."

"Where does that leave us then?" Zumwald asked.

"The field office is talking to the suspects again," Buzz shrugged. "But they feel the information they got from them is accurate and that they have told them everything they know. The mercenaries believe that they were working for this unknown terrorist group."

The captain leafed through the report. "We do have one small lead, however, though I don't know if it's worth a hell of a lot. It says here that the examination of the plastic explosive residue gathered from the various damaged facilities shows that it all came from the same manufacturing plant in England."

"How do they know that?" Wolff asked.

"The chemicals that make up plastic explosive can be coded," Buzz explained. "Something about mixing an inert material in with the explosive. When it is detonated, these inert molecules remain behind as a residue and can be identified."

"Anyway," Buzz continued. "Langley queried Scotland Yard and they reported that the particular lot of explosives in question was initially purchased by United Petroleum, Ltd. However, it was later reported stolen from the company's docks in Kuwait."

"And just who's this United Petroleum outfit?" Zumwald asked.

"It says here that they're a major British oil producing firm with operations all over the world."

"By any chance, are any of their operations in our neighborhood?"

"I'll have to check on that," Buzz said. "But that's about all we have for now."

"That sure as hell doesn't give us much to work with," Zumwald said, looking disgusted.

Buzz looked thoughtful for a moment. "Actually, it gives us our first connection," he said quietly.

"What's that, sir?"

"Kuwait," Buzz answered. "The plastique was stolen there and the mercs were recruited there."

"But I thought the report said that the mercs were all Australians and South Africans?" Zumwald asked. "What were they doing in Kuwait?"

"That's a long story," Buzz replied. "To start with, Kuwait used to be a British protectorate and, even when the Brits gave the place back to the rightful owners, many British Army officers stayed behind to advise the Kuwaiti army. Over the years, the place has become a haven for expatriate Brits and Europeans working the mercenary trade, particularly South Africans when their country was overrun."

Everyone in the room vividly remembered the scenes they had watched on the television of the fall of South Africa in the mid-90's. The death and destruction had been the most terrible anyone had seen since the worst days of the Tet offensive in the Vietnam War or the Cambodian civil war. Cut off from all support by the Western nations, the embattled white South Africans had fought valiantly against the overwhelming hordes of black nationalists well armed by their new allies, the Red Chinese and the North Koreans.

Since most of the survivors knew no other trade than that of making war, South African men quickly swelled the ranks

76

of the growing international mercenary community and had fought in every brush fire war since then.

"So," Buzz said. "What we have is the mercenaries, the explosives and the oil company all coming together in the same place at the same time. It's paper thin, I know, but it's all we have right now."

"But an oil company blowing up oil rigs doesn't make sense to me, Captain."

"Maybe it does, though," Buzz said thoughtfully. "Granted it's a long shot, but I think I need to look into that British outfit and find out what they've been doing since the Arab-Israeli War."

"What do you mean?" Wolff asked.

"It wasn't only the Arab oil companies who got put out of business when the Israelis nuked their oil fields," Buzz explained. "There were quite a few European companies who depended on the OPEC countries for their crude oil and, when the Middle Eastern fields were contaminated, they lost their oil supplies too."

"But what does that have to do with the new oil fields in the Gulf, sir?"

"That's what I don't know," Buzz frowned. "But I think I know how I can find out." He pushed the button to the intercom on his desk.

"Yes, sir," Ruby answered the intercom from the outer office.

"Put me through to the investigative branch at Washington headquarters."

"Yes, sir," Mom answered. "Do you want it on the scrambler?"

Buzz thought for a moment. "Yes, please."

A few seconds later, Mom came back on the intercom. "I've got your call on scramcomm."

Buzz picked up the phone on his desk and switched it over to the scrambled communications mode. "Doc, this is Buzz Corcran down in Texas . . . Yeah, I'm fine. Yourself? . . . Look, could you do a little research for me? . . . Yeah, we're trying to get this Gulf of Mexico thing under control and we're running into a brick wall. Can you check out a British firm for me? United Petroleum, Limited."

He flipped through the CIA report. "Their home office is in Manchester. I'd like to get a general rundown on their activities for the last couple of years and I need to know if they've had any contacts with American oil companies in this area in, say the last year or so? . . . Good, I'll be waiting to hear from you."

Buzz hung up the phone. "Even if they are clean," he said. "We need to check them out so we can quit worrying about them."

"What do we do in the meantime?" Wolff asked.

"Just SOS," Buzz replied with a shrug. "Same Old Shit. We keep on patrolling and hope we get lucky again. I know it's not much, but it's all we can do right now."

"I hope something breaks pretty soon," Wolff grumbled. "I'm getting calluses on my ass from flying around in circles all day."

"You could be back in Denver freezing your ass off while you scraped ice off your rotor blades right now."

"At least I'd know what in the hell I was doing," the pilot said. "Here, I haven't a clue."

Chapter 12

Cunningham Oil Company, Houston, Texas

Travis Cunningham III read the decoded message for a third time before wadding it into a ball and dropping it into the security disposal unit at the end of his oak desk. A brief flash of flame and an electric whine assured him that the message had been incinerated and the ashes ground to powder.

The short, stocky oil executive swiveled around in his chair and stared out the window of his suite on the 30th floor in the Cunningham Building at the city spread out below. As the year 1999 drew to a close, Houston was once more a boom town, more like it had been in the early seventies than what it had been in the late eighties. The discovery of the new Gulf oil fields in the mid-nineties had revitalized the city. Once more, oil was king in Texas and the king lived in Houston.

This new prosperity, however, was not being shared by the owner of Cunningham Oil. The building still bore his grandfather's name, the legendary Travis Cunningham the First, but Travis Cunningham III had been reduced to leasing his office space in it. He had had to sell the building a long time ago just to keep the family business afloat when the oil market collapsed in 1982. Like many of the smaller family-held, independent oil companies back then, Cunningham had been badly overextended and had been able to hang on only by the skin of its teeth. Since then, the only thing that had kept the company solvent were their two remaining offshore oil derricks and a few marginal, outdated refineries.

The discovery of the new oil fields in the Gulf might have revitalized Houston and the Texas oil business, but it had brought no change to the fortunes of Cunningham Oil. The big strike had been discovered at the edge of the old Cunningham offshore leases, but he had not been able to tap into it. The leases in the new field had been snapped up by companies with enough development capital on hand to bid for and develop the field and Cunningham Oil with its marginal cash flow had been out in the cold.

A few months earlier, the company had been on the verge of bankruptcy again when a representative of the British oil giant, United Petroleum, Limited, stopped by Houston and presented Cunningham with an interesting proposition.

They wanted to buy Cunningham Oil, lock stock and barrel.

At first Cunningham had been suspicious, he had never really liked Brits anyway, they always acted so damned superior. And as a Texan he had been right up front about his suspicions.

"Why would a big company like United want anything to do with a piss ant little outfit like Cunningham?" he asked United's representative.

The impeccably dressed Brit smiled. "We don't actually," he said bluntly. "We just want your American address so we can do business here. We really want access to the new Gulf oil fields."

Cunningham had been stunned, but it made sense. The new field was within the 200 mile economic limit of American waters. The federal offshore drilling regulations gave first bid to American based firms and effectively squeezed out foreign oil companies, including United Petroleum.

The proposal the Brit laid out was risky, but Cunningham's reward would be an executive's "Golden Parachute" to end all "Golden Parachutes." If he could pull it off, the day that United Petroleum took over Cunningham Oil, Travis Cunningham III would retire with enough money to last him the rest of his life.

But for that to happen, he had to do something immediately about the information he had just received in the coded message. United Petroleum's intelligence network was better than those of many nations and he had just been warned that the federal authorities were inquiring into his company's affairs. Particularly his rumored business connection with United.

Cunningham turned back to his desk and punched in a code to activate the modem on the computer built into his desk. Flipping up the monitor and pulling out the keyboard, he quickly typed in a phone number.

The modem dialed the number and within two rings, the screen came alive. The words "Go ahead" appeared.

"This is Mister Smith." Cunningham typed.

"What kind of Smith?" the screen requested.

"Condor," he typed.

"This is Falcon, go ahead," the screen answered.

"I have just learned that the Federal Tac Force has become very interested in my company's operations," the oilman typed. "I want you to advance the next attack to November ninth at twenty hundred hours. The target will be the Cunningham refinery Number Two at Littlefield."

"Are you sure that you want to do that?" Falcon asked.

"Do you have a problem with that?"

"No," Falcon answered. "I can delay the planned mission on November eleventh and shift that team to cover it."

"Contact Eagle to get the Tac Force patrol schedule," Cunningham typed. "I don't want your people to run into them again."

The unexpected capture of the seven mercenaries had been a very close thing, too close. Fortunately for the sake of the plan, the pilots had been killed and the others knew nothing of what they were really doing.

"Anything further?" Falcon asked.

"No. Condor out."

Cunningham killed the modem connection and sat back in his chair. A thin smile crossed his face. That should get the Tac Police off his back for good. The next site that would be hit by the "Vengeance of God" terrorists would be one of his own oil refineries. Not even the Tac Police would think that a businessman would destroy one of his own production facilities.

It was an older refinery that was bleeding red ink all over the balance sheets anyway, but the Tac Cops wouldn't know that. All they would know was that Cunningham Oil had also suffered a loss in this latest wave of Arab terrorist bombings. The insurance would pay for the damage to the plant and United would pay him for any uncovered losses he incurred. He couldn't lose.

It was a good thing, he thought, that there was no shortage of wild eyed, fanatic Arabs who still harbored a burning hatred for anything Western. They made the perfect cover story for this operation, no one would ever question that they were behind it. If the radical Arabs ever came to their senses and started acting like civilized humans, the Western nations would have to invent someone to take their place as the international villains.

Cunningham hit the intercom button on the phone and his secretary answered instantly.

"Miss Sally," he said. "Get me the security supervisor at the Littlefield plant will you."

"Right away, Mister Cunningham."

He leaned back in his chair and waited for the man to come on the line. In just a few minutes, this little problem would be taken care of.

"J.B. Bonner," the voice on the phone speaker said.

"Bonner, this is Travis Cunningham . . ."

"There it is," Wolff said as he banked the Griffin over to circle the Cunningham refinery facility at Littlefield, Texas. "We're right on time."

The small coastal refinery looked very much like all the others they had patrolled that afternoon. A man wearing blue jeans and a khaki shirt stepped out from a small building by the main gate and waved at the cops in the circling Griffin. All was well.

"Everything looks fine from up here," Mugabe said as he checked the site off on their patrol sheet and logged in their arrival time.

"Where's the next stop?" the pilot asked.

"Just head south and fly down the coastline," Mugabe said. "Rockport, Texas, the last stop before we turn back. Those guys on One Three say that they have real good catfish and hush puppies there, you want to stop in for dinner while we're there?"

"Sure," Wolff shrugged as he banked the Griffin over to the new heading. "Why not, I'll call us in Code Seven for thirty when we get there."

"I don't see how you guys can stand this," Cuervo spoke

up. "I've only spent a couple of hours flying up and down the coast and making sure that no one has blown something up and I'm going crazy already. How much longer are you going to have to do this?"

"Beats the shit outa me," Wolff growled. "Until someone can get a fix on these bastards, though, there's not a hell of a lot else we can do but keep on looking for them."

"Maybe something will break soon," Cuervo said.

"I sure as hell hope so," Wolff said. "This is driving me batshit."

"But," Mugabe broke in. "We're getting to try out a lot of great restaurants."

Wolff was going back for a second helping of hush puppies and cole slaw when the personal communicator on his belt started buzzing. Thumbing the switch on, he brought it to his lips. "You have reached the Wolfman," he said. "I am having dinner right now, so leave a message at the tone and I will get right back to you. Beep."

"This is Dragon Control," Mom's raspy voice sounded tinny on the small speaker of the communicator. "The Cunningham refinery at Littlefield has just been hit. Command One wants you there ASAP. How copy."

Wolff laid his plate down on the table. "This is One Zero, we're rolling now."

As they approached the burning refinery, the scene from the air was one of utter chaos. Sheets of flame leaped up into the night sky and the flashing red lights of fire trucks and emergency vehicles cast an eerie glimmer of light, illuminating the dozens of people scrambling to get the raging fire under control. Wolff brought the Griffin down to a careful landing off the side of the main access road to the plant and shut the turbines down.

The two chopper cops quickly checked in with the local authorities to get the story on what had happened. Not surprisingly, as had been the pattern so far, there was little that anyone could tell them. The terrorists had come in through the fence on the back side, planted their explosive charges and had made their escape. The only thing that was different this time was that they had been observed by some of the plant's workers. And, when they had tried to interfere, the terrorists had opened up on them before running away.

While Wolff talked to the sheriff, Mugabe saw an ambulance crew carrying a stretcher out of the wreckage. Another paramedic was following them and Mugabe stopped him. "How many people got hurt?' he asked the paramedic.

"We got two pretty bad burn cases," the man answered. "Maybe three and one guy got shot."

"Is he dead?"

"Nope." The medic shook his head. "Not yet, but he's hurt real bad and I don't know if he's gonna make it. He took a round in the spine."

"Shit."

Mugabe looked around at the wreckage of the refinery. Whoever was behind this, the stakes had just gotten bigger. Finally someone on the sidelines had gotten hurt and the pressure to get this stopped fast was going to escalate.

Chapter 13

Bolen Air Base

Buzz was in the TOC talking with Ruby Jenkins when the report about the attack on the Cunningham refinery came in over the radio.

"Shit," he said, shaking his head. "There goes that theory."

Earlier that afternoon he had received a call back from the Washington headquarters with information about a rumored connection between United Petroleum and Cunningham Oil, but the oil industry grapevine said that a buyout was still in the works. And a listing of the rigs that had been hit showed that Cunningham Oil was the only outfit that had not had at least one of their facilities damaged.

"What theory, Buzz?" Mom asked, looking up from her communication's console.

"Oh, nothing," he said.

"Run it past me anyway. Your hunches have a better batting average than most."

TPF Sergeant Ruby Jenkins hadn't always been known as Mom. At one time, she had been one of the nation's top undercover policewomen. She had been one of the first female special agents in the DEA and had made a name for herself on dangerous undercover assignments against terrorist and drug operations. Her reputation for tackling difficult jobs had been crowned when she had tracked down the terrorist gang who had killed California's governor and his anti-war activist wife in one of the most celebrated political assassinations of the early nineties.

The unwelcome international publicity that had resulted from her successful investigation, however, had worked against her. While on her next assignment, her cover was blown and she had almost been killed when a major drug bust went bad. When she got out of the hospital, she had been reassigned to a boring desk job and had been about to go out of her mind, when Buzz recruited her to become his operations sergeant for Dragon Flight.

Buzz had learned to trust her steel trap mind and he often discussed his ideas with her. She wouldn't have survived as long as she had working undercover without having a well-developed knack for picking up on little things that others had missed.

"It's not much," he said. "Just a rumor that one of the small independent oil companies was approached by that British firm to talk about a buyout."

"Why would the Brits want an outfit like that?"

Buzz looked thoughtful for a moment, "That's what I

can't figure out." He sat down on the edge of Mom's console. "In fact, I can't figure any of this out. This whole story of Arab revenge in the United States for something that happened years ago in the Middle East, just doesn't make any sense. Particularly when the CIA can't pick up any leads about this so called 'Vengeance of God' organization. I know those people have long memories, but this is ridiculous."

"So," Mom broke in. "You've been looking somewhere else for an answer."

"Yeah," he said thoughtfully. "Something local. Something more normal. You know, something like greed, a fast buck, that sort of thing."

Mom laughed. "Something that you can understand?"

Buzz grinned. "Well, you know me," he said. "I'm just a simple flyer at heart."

"Bullshit."

Buzz laughed.

Buzz Corcran had been a young, hot rock, Huey gunship pilot with the 1st Air Cav in the Vietnam War and had picked up his nickname when he had made a high speed, low level run over the Division HQs at An Khe after returning from a very successful mission. Unfortunately, he had made his run right over the general's personal latrine and the general had been on his throne when the rotor blast had tipped it over. Corcran had been lucky that he hadn't spent the rest of his tour picking up cigarette butts along the Ho Chi Minh trail.

Two tours in the Air Cav and four Purple Hearts later, he had finally decided that he needed to find a less exciting occupation while he still could. He resigned his commission from the Army and went into the helicopter maintenance business in California. After a year of that, though, he was bored out of his mind and had answered an ad recruiting chopper pilots for the California State Highway Patrol. It turned out that cruising up and down the crowded freeways looking for speeders wasn't exciting enough for him either and he soon joined up as a pilot with the Federal Drug Enforcement Agency.

When President Bush's war on drugs had heated up a couple of years after the successful invasion of Panama, Buzz had led the first contingent of DEA gunships into Colombia and Peru to do battle with the cocaine barons and their private armies when the civilian governments in that region finally collapsed. Corcran had been in his natural element there, fighting guerrillas in the tangled tropical jungles.

When the Tac Force had been formed in 1996, Buzz transferred over from the DEA and had been chosen to command the first Dragon Flight. He enjoyed running his unit, but he resented having to be deskbound most of the time. At heart he was still a pilot first and each year he somehow managed to wrangle enough hours behind the controls of one of the Griffins to keep his flight status active and the gold police pilot wings he proudly wore brightly polished.

"What do you mean?"

"Even though we have foreign mercenaries running around blowing things up," Mom explained. "This still feels like a local affair to me."

"That makes two of us," Buzz agreed. "All I have to do now is to find out who in the hell is really behind this."

"Maybe it's as simple as someone being pissed off at his boss."

Buzz laughed. "Everyone's pissed off at their bosses, even the boys and girls of Dragon Flight. If I followed that theory, ninety percent of the people in the oil industry would be on our suspect list."

"Maybe that's where you should start—with the oil companies."

The next two days passed quickly for Dragon Flight. After the Cunningham incident, Buzz had increased the patrols, but all he accomplished was to exhaust his flight crews. Even with the increased TPF presence, two more facilities had been hit. Both times the attacks had come immediately after the Griffins had checked in with them and reported to the TOC that they were okay.

The crushed oyster shell parking lot in front of the Ravon Inn at Littlefield, Texas, was packed with pickup trucks, old Trans Am Pontiacs and the occasional Toyota or Honda. It was Friday night and the five man band inside was hammering out country and western favorites with their amplifiers cranked up as far as they would go. They weren't all that good, but they were loud and they were live. It was hard to find a holoband playing anywhere in Texas on a Friday or Saturday night. Texans liked their music loud and live.

Many of the tavern's patrons were sitting in their cars and pickups in the parking lot drinking their Lone Star long necks in the open air. The music was loud enough that they didn't miss a note and it was easier than trying to fight their way inside for a table. Also, when they had to recycle a little of that Lone Star beer, they wouldn't have to elbow their way back to the crowded rest rooms. They could just crawl out of their trucks, stagger to the back bumper and water the crushed oyster shell.

Most of the parking lot drinkers had a buddy along, but one man sat alone in his pickup keeping one eye on the front door and the other on the white Chevy with the Cunningham Oil badge on the door. Judson Williams slowly took a sip of his beer as he watched the door, his hand resting on the jack handle lying on the seat beside him. He remembered once reading in a car magazine where some Yankee journalist had called fighting with tire irons the southern form of interpretive dance. Well, he was going to put on one hell of a dance show here tonight as soon as he caught up with J.B. Bonner.

Jud Williams had been a foreman at the Cunningham refinery in Littlefield for the last ten years. And until just two nights ago, his son, Jud Junior, had followed in his footsteps as an oilman. Now the boy lay in a hospital bed with a bullet in his back and J.B. Bonner, the refinery's security chief, had a little explaining to do.

In the aftermath of the terrorist attack, Jud had tried to run an investigation of the incident himself. He just didn't understand how the terrorists had been able to penetrate the plant security so easily. At first he had dry-holed, until he talked to Roy LeFevere, an old friend who worked in the security section.

LeFevere told him that they had come through the section of the fence where the security monitors had been temporarily turned off for maintenance. He said that the orders to turn the cameras off had come down from Bonner, but that he didn't understand why it had been done. He hadn't seen anything wrong with them.

Jud took another pull on the Lone Star and glanced at his watch, turning it so he could read the dial in the light from the neon sign. Bonner should be coming out in another fifteen minutes or so. The security chief never stayed in the tavern much past eleven o'clock. He talked big, but everybody knew that he was afraid to be out drinking too late because his old lady would kick his ass when he got home.

The door opened and a man stepped out into the dimly lit parking lot. Jud opened the door of his pickup and, holding the jack handle down at his side, moved to intercept him. "J.B.!" he called out, "Wait up! I need to have a word with ya'll."

Bonner was a big man. When he was younger he had been big and muscular, but now he was just big. Williams, on the other hand, looked like a strong wind could blow him away. That was just one of the two reasons why he had the jack handle in his hand. The other one was that he knew J.B. Bonner from a long way back.

Bonner stopped and squinted to see who it was. "That you, Jud?" he called out. "What'n the hell you doing out here?"

"Gotta talk to you."

" 'Bout what?"

" 'Bout my boy, Jud Junior," Wilson said. "You know he got hurt pretty bad the other night."

"Yeah and I was real sorry to hear about that, Jud. He's a good boy."

"Well, he's got a bullet in his back and the doctors can't tell me if he'll ever walk again."

"I sure am sorry," Bonner said, shaking his head. "But to be honest with you, Jud, I don't rightly see how that pertains to me."

"Well, J.B.", Williams said rocking back on his heels, "It pertains to your telling the security people to shut down the monitors the other night."

"Where'd ya'll hear that, Jud," Bonner's eyes narrowed. "Who you been talking to anyway?"

The security chief slowly dropped his left hand to his back pants pocket. Like a striking snake, Williams whipped the jack handle up and brought it down across the top of Bonner's left shoulder. The crack of his breaking collar bone could not be heard above the music, but his scream was. A big folding blade knife fell from the nerveless fingers of his left hand as the security chief went down to his knees.

"Ya'll shouldn't have done that," Williams said, scooping up the knife and stuffing it in his back pocket. "You forget that I knew you was left-handed."

"What the fuck you think you're doing, Jud?" Bonner groaned.

"Like I said," Williams slapped the palm of his hand with the jack handle. "I need to talk to you 'bout them security monitors."

"I ain't telling you shit, boy," Bonner snapped. "You'd better get the fuck outa here 'fore the sheriff shows up and puts your ass in jail to sober up."

"You want me to call him for ya?" Williams asked.

Bonner struggled back to his feet, his useless left hand held in his right, but he didn't say a word.

"I didn't think so," Williams smiled grimly. He took the big man by the arm and led him over to his pickup. "You need to sit down for a spell, J.B." he said, as he opened the passenger side door. "That arm's probably killin' ya."

Chapter 14

Bolen Air Base

The comm unit on Corcran's desk came to life. Buzz looked up from the report he was reading and pushed the intercom button. "Yeah."

"Captain," came Mom's voice. "There's a man out here to see you."

"Who is it?"

"A Mister Judson Williams. He says that he's a foreman at the Cunningham refinery in Littlefield that got hit the other night."

This was just what he needed today, to have to waste his time listening to a citizen's complaint about the Tac Force not doing their job. He already had been barraged with calls from Washington complaining about the same thing. "I'm pretty busy right now, Ruby, what does he want?"

"He says he has information about who was behind the attack."

Buzz put his head in his hands. This was even worse than a complaint, a citizen who had solved the crime. Every time something big went down, everybody and his pet frog had to tell the cops their theory about who did it. "Tell him to talk to Zumwald about it."

"I did sir," Mom answered. "But he says that he won't talk to anyone but you, Captain."

He released the intercom button for a moment, "Shit!" he muttered. "Okay," he called out. "Send him in."

A tall, thin man in faded jeans, scuffed boots and a blue

work shirt walked into the office. He was holding a sweat-stained cowboy hat in his hands. "Capt'n," he said, holding out a calloused hand. "I'm Jud Williams."

"Buzz Corcran," Buzz said, standing up and taking the man's hand. "Have a seat, Mister Williams. I understand that you have something to tell me."

Wilson sat down. "I'm sorry to take your time, Capt'n, but it's like this. My boy got shot up pretty bad in the attack the other night."

"I'm sorry to hear that," Buzz said automatically.

Wilson continued as if he hadn't heard. "Anyway, I started looking around on my own, trying to find out what had happened. I didn't learn much."

No shit, Buzz thought.

"Then I went to see ol' Roy LeFevere in plant security and I asked him why them terrorists got in without anyone knowing about it. Shoot, we got them television cameras all over that place. Even a jackrabbit can't get in there without being seen."

The foreman leaned forward in his chair. "Well, he up and tells me that right before the attack, J.B. Bonner called and told him to turn off half of the monitors."

Suddenly Buzz was interested. "Who's this Bonner?" he asked writing the man's name down.

"He's the plant security chief."

"Okay, go on," Buzz prompted him. "Why did he order that?"

"Well, ole Roy told me that J.B. gave him some cock and bull story 'bout needing to pull some maintenance on the cameras. But Roy swore that there weren't nothin' wrong with them cameras."

Buzz sat back in his chair. He had been right after all, there was something funny going on with Cunningham Oil. "Why do you think Bonner did that?" he asked calmly, trying to keep the excitement off his face.

"Well, Capt'n, that's what I decided I wanted to find out." Williams smiled thinly. He paused for a moment as if to consider how much he should tell the federal cop. "The next night see, I went on down to the Ravon Inn right outside of town, that's where most of the boys from the plant go to hoot it up on a Saturday night, and I caught up with ole J.B. Well sir, we had us a little talk and he told me that he had gotten a call from Mister Travis Cunningham hisself to shut them cameras down.''

"That's very interesting," Buzz said. "Did this Bonner have any idea why Mister Cunningham wanted him to do something like that?"

"He didn't rightly say," Williams admitted. "But I got a bad feeling about it, Capt'n."

Buzz thought for a moment. "Are you willing to sign a statement about what you've just told me?"

"Sure thing," the foreman said.

"Also, we'd like to know anything you can tell us about Bonner and Cunningham himself."

"No problem with Bonner, Capt'n, me and ole J.B. has been friends for a long time." He paused and his jaw set. "Leastways we were till my boy got hurt. But, Mister Cunningham, I don't know much about him, 'cept that he sure as hell ain't the man his daddy was."

"How's that?"

"Well, Travis Cunningham the second, was a man's man, you know what I mean. He'd shake your hand and look you right in the eye. His son, well, he's always been a sneaky little bastard. I never did trust him."

Bingo, Buzz thought. If you want to know something about a man, ask the guys who work for him.

Buzz got to his feet and held his hand out. "Thanks for coming in, Mister Williams. The clerk outside will take your statement."

The minute Williams was gone, Buzz got on the phone to the TPF's Houston field office.

Travis Cunningham's face paled under his tan as he read the fax that had just come in from Washington. Goddamn that redneck Bonner. Of all the people to have turned against him, he never should have trusted him. He crumpled the fax sheet and incinerated it.

His plan had come so damned close to working. Another month or two and he would have gained control of the Mega-platform and would have been able to retire for life. He had thought that plan was foolproof, but obviously it had not been foolproof enough. Now instead of living the good life in Brazil or Argentina, he would be lucky if he could stay out of a federal prison.

Damn! He was so close.

The Megaplatform Cunningham was after was the brain child of Bo Starr, the crafty old bastard who ran Starr Oil, another of the few remaining independent Texas oilmen. Unlike the Cunningham operation, Starr specialized in oil exploration and it had finally paid off in a big way. It had been Starr's geologists who had discovered the massive new oil field some 180 miles out into the Gulf.

This new discovery was situated deep beneath an old played out oil field and everyone in the industry had thought that old Starr had finally lost his mind when he bought up all the leases in the area he could get his hands on. It had taken almost all of his capital to secure the leases, but when it was done, he announced the discovery of the new field a half a mile under the old depleted substrata.

Starr was smart, he had to give him that. Rather than trying to work the field with his own limited resources, he kept control of all the leases and had sub-leased them to the major companies to build what soon became the world's largest oil drilling complex, the Megaplatform. This was an offshore city of deep water drilling rigs and collection and refinery facilities built in close proximity so that all operations from sinking the wells to transferring the petroleum to the super tankers could take place in one location.

The Megaplatform was the greatest money maker in the history of the American oil industry, but it was vulnerable. By holding onto all the leases himself, Starr was making money hand over fist from the royalties, but he was also principally responsible for any environmental damage that might result from the operation.

With the passage of the Exxon Valdez Act in 1993, oil companies could be held responsible for any damage caused by any oil-related accident. And, with the lesson of the disastrous Alaskan spill caused by the bill's namesake, the law now stipulated that the oil companies responsible for the damage deposit three times the estimated cost of clean-up into a special environmental protection fund within ten days of the accident. Failure to do so would result in the immediate seizure of the company's assets and their immediate sale to cover the amount of money not deposited.

It was a good bill. Under its provisions, an oil company could never again get away with destroying the environment and then just walking away from it as had happened in Alaska in the '80s. But, not surprisingly, none of the bill's sponsors had ever taken terrorist actions against oil companies into consideration when it had been written. There was no provision for letting a company off the hook when terrorists blew up their facilities.

Starr Oil was making a pile of money, but much of it had already been posted as a bond for the damage already done to their facilities at other locations. A few more terrorist attacks and the company's assets, including the leases for the oil under the Megaplatform, would have to go on the auction block to cover the clean up costs and that was where Cunningham had planned to come in.

With the unlimited financial backing United Petroleum planned to provide him, Cunningham would buy up the leases and take over the operation of the Megaplatform. He would have virtually no competition in the bidding because all the other oil companies had their assets tied up controlling damage to their rigs as well. Once this was accomplished, his company would quietly be acquired by the British oil giant and the biggest oil field in the United States would be owned by a foreign company.

On the day that happened, Travis Cunningham III would

have become America's latest multi-billionaire and would have permanently retired from the oil business.

Now, however, it looked like the whole plan was out the window. At least that's what the fax sheet in his hand indicated. The senator who was on United Oil's payroll had warned him that the Tac Force had arrested J.B. Bonner and had learned that Cunningham had ordered the attack on his own refinery in Littlefield.

He activated the modem on his desk computer. He only had a few hours, if that, before the police stormed into his office to arrest him, but he had a few calls to make before he disappeared.

Cunningham had never really trusted the Brits and had worked up a little fall-back plan of his own in case something like this did happen. One way or the other, he was still going to retire with his quarter billion dollars, it was just going to be a little more difficult now.

It was helpful that the Brits in the pin-striped suits who ran United Petroleum had wanted to keep their hands completely clean of this whole affair. They had left all the dirty work to Cunningham so that they could not be connected with him if anything went wrong. This also meant that they had no way to contact Falcon and his mercenaries, which meant that they had no way to stop Cunningham from changing the plan and collecting his payoff anyway.

The computer screen came alive and the words, "Go ahead" appeared.

"This is Mister Smith," the oil man typed.

"What kind of Smith?"

"Condor."

"This is Falcon, go ahead."

When the officers from the Houston field office arrived at the Cunningham building an hour later armed with a federal warrant for the arrest of Travis Cunningham III, he was gone. His secretary told the federal cops that he had told her he was taking the rest of the day off.

* * *

As dusk fell that evening, Travis Cunningham III stepped out of his private jet onto a dirt airstrip cut into the jungles of the Mexican Yuacatan peninsula. Waiting to meet him was the Arab known only as Falcon.

"You should not have come here," the mercenary leader snapped, his anger darkening his usually calm face. "It's too dangerous. If this plan is to work, there can be no connection between us."

"There's been a change in the plans," Cunningham said, looking beyond the Arab to the camouflaged figures of mercenaries waiting in line for their evening meal. "We've got to talk."

"About what?"

"There have been problems," Cunningham said. "We have to step up the campaign."

Falcon looked at his employer for a long moment. "Come with me," he said and turned to walk toward a small building hidden under the trees.

Falcon could well believe that there had been problems. The first and only time he had met Cunningham a few months ago, he had not been impressed. In his twenty-odd years in the mercenary trade, he had worked for many kinds of employers, some had been strong men and some had been weak.

Falcon prided himself on being able to tell a man's character by his eyes, and Cunningham was weak.

Chapter 15

The Gulf of Mexico

At night, a hundred and eighty miles out in the Gulf of Mexico, the Megaplatform looked like a small floating city from the air. The blazing lights from the fourteen separate facilities that made up the complex lit the skies for miles around and turned night into day. Natural gas collected from the oil wells powered several electric generators, so there was no need to conserve power. Even at four o'clock in the morning, the lights blazed.

The centerpiece of this floating city was the central collection platform. This, the largest of the fourteen structures, was the supply base as well as the administrative center for all the other platforms, as well as housing the dispensary and the communications center on the top floor of the structure. It also served as the focal point for the off-duty activities of the hundreds of oil workers who manned the floating city. To keep the men entertained on their off-duty hours the Megaplatform was also equipped with a nightclub on the platform, a restaurant, the company store, a library and video music room.

The Megaplatform was so self contained that some of the men were known to spend their vacation days there rather than go ashore and spend their hard earned money in the expensive honky tonks and bars lining the dock sides of the Texas oil towns.

The Megaplatform even had its own security force, but they were not armed with anything more powerful than nightsticks. No firearms of any kind were allowed around so much inflammable material.

* * *

Four French built Aerospatiale Super Puma helicopters flew low to the water, well under the air traffic control radar in the Megaplatform's small control tower. The navigation lights were turned off and the matt dark green finish on the machines made them invisible against the night sky. The pilots flew with their instruments and night vision goggles, but when they were ten miles out from the platform, the sky was so bright that they took off the goggles and flew the rest of the way on VFR.

As the choppers neared the floating city, two of the dark green ships veered off from their companions and headed for the multi-million gallon oil containment facility next to the central control platform. Still keeping close to the water, the two remaining choppers continued on to the central platform in the middle of the complex. One of the ships popped up just long enough to let off a team of four men on the deserted back side of the platform well away from the sleepy commo watch officer on duty in the control tower.

The four men, their faces blackened with night camouflage paint, raced across the deck for the stairwell leading up to the control room. Their rubber-soled boots made no noise as they ran up the stairs. At the top of the stairs, they halted and took gas masks from the pouches on their equipment belts. After donning the masks, two of the men pulled grenades from their ammo belts and pulled the pins.

Snapping the control room door open, they tossed the grenades in and slammed it shut after them. The radio operator barely had time to look up before the grenades popped and released the gas. He slumped over his radio console, unconscious.

After counting to thirty, the mercenaries opened the door again and moved in. Stepping up to the window looking out over the helipad, one of the mercenaries took a flashlight from his belt. Aiming it at the window, he snapped the beam on and off three times.

The helipad on the central platform was big enough to

accommodate two of the Super Pumas at once and they quickly set down side by side. No sooner had their skids touched down than the rear doors slid open disgorging two twelve man assault teams. The mercenaries quickly fanned out, their assault rifles at the ready.

At the oil collection platform, one of the other ships touched down to offload its assault team. The other chopper did the same at the rig next to it.

Oil field workers aren't known for rolling over and playing dead, but, unarmed, sleepy oil rig workers were no match for fast moving, heavily armed professional soldiers. There were no serious casualties among the workers.

As soon as one platform was secure, the choppers would land and take the mercenaries not needed to guard their captives and fly to the next one to secure it. In less than thirty minutes, the Megaplatform was completely in the hands of the mercenaries.

Dawn over the Megaplatform was spectacular and the breaking day found all of the fourteen platforms well secured by Falcon's men. The few oil men who had escaped the roundup last night were quickly tracked down and added to the bag of prisoners.

Falcon rapidly sorted out his catch, he kept the managerial staff, and released the men who actually did the work. Rounding up two of the lumbering supply boats that kept the Megaplatform stocked, he had most of the oil men loaded into them. After destroying the ship's radios, he ordered the captains of the vessels to set sail for the nearest port. He warned them to not even think about turning back, quietly explaining that if they tried anything foolish, they would be blown out of the water without further warning.

As Falcon had expected, neither one of the ships turned back.

As soon as the supply boats were dots on the horizon, the Arab known only as Falcon went looking for Cunningham and found him behind the consoles in the control room. "The workers are gone," he reported.

"Good," Cunningham grinned and rubbed his hands together like a schoolboy who had successfully pulled a prank on one of his teachers. "Now we can get down to business."

"And what is that?

"You will now place another call as the 'Vengeance of God' and demand a ransom for the return of the Mega-platform."

Falcon hesitated and Cunningham continued. "Believe me, it's the last call you'll have to make."

"I still do not like this idea," Falcon frowned. "It it too dangerous. When we do that, the Tac Force will respond and it is risky to go up against them."

"What are they going to do?" Cunningham laughed almost hysterically. "Risk a multi-billion dollar investment for pocket change? They don't dare try to stop us. And, even if they did," his eyes gleamed. "We have enough fire-power to blow them out of the sky."

"I still don't like it."

"Do you want to collect your money?"

"That's what it states in the contract." Falcon's voice was controlled. The mercenary life depended on contracts being honored. Falcon had already been paid half a million dollars to put his team together and was due the other half when the operation was over. He had kept his half of the bargain and he did not like to hear this man treating him as if he were an amateur. If anyone connected with this operation was an amateur, it was Cunningham.

"Well," Cunningham said, as he handed him a sheet of paper. "This is the only way that you're going to get it. And, when payday comes, there'll be a little extra something in the envelope for you. We're going for a billion dollars and five million of it will be yours."

Silently, Falcon reached for the paper.

Making certain that the radio was tuned to the international emergency frequency, Cunningham pressed the switch to activate the microphone and handed it to Falcon. "Here," he said. "Read the message."

Falcon glanced at the message and then back to Cunningham, his expression unreadable. After a moment, he reached for the microphone.

"This is the Vengeance of God," the Arab read in his distinctively accented voice. "We are now in total control of the Megaplatform and are holding most of the staff hostage. As long as the authorities keep away, no one will be hurt and the facilities will not be damaged. But if any attempt is made to re-take the platform, we are ready to release the crude oil from the holding tanks into the Gulf and destroy the facility as well.

"Our demands are simple, we are holding the Megaplatform ransom for one billion dollars. We do not care who puts up the money for the ransom, either the capitalists or the government, but if you want this facility intact, you will comply with this demand. If not, we will leave it a burning wreck in the water surrounded by the world's largest oil slick.

"The money is due in three days and, as soon as it is ready, contact us on this frequency for further instructions. This the 'Vengeance of God'."

Cunningham smiled triumphantly as Falcon laid the microphone down. It was done. Now all he had to do was to wait. Literally, he had them over a barrel, several million barrels in fact. He smiled at his own pun; they would have to give him the money now.

High over the Gulf coast of Texas, the sharklike shape of Dragon One Zero cruised through the clear blue morning sky. Wolff, Mugabe and Cuervo had the early morning patrol again. The pilot was just starting his descent to check out their next facility when Mom's raspy voice broke in over the command frequency.

"All Dragon units," she radioed. "This is Dragon Control, return to base immediately."

Wolff keyed his throat mike. "Control, this is One Zero," he radioed. "Good copy. What's up?"

"One Zero, this is Control," she answered. "For the last time, this is not a secure channel, you will be briefed when you arrive."

"Wonder what Mom's got her tit in a wringer about today?" the pilot muttered, as he banked the chopper over and set their course back to Bolen Air Base.

"Maybe we're finally being recalled home?" Mugabe said hopefully.

"Fat chance of that," Wolff replied. "The way this thing's developing, we're all going to retire down here."

Since the one skirmish Wolff and Mugabe had with the terrorists had been on the first day they had arrived, there had been no further contact with them. There had been no shortage of terrorist incidents, but the chopper cops had been unable to do anything to prevent them. The terrorists only hit when the sky was clear of Griffins and Wolff was beginning to think that someone was leaking their patrol schedule to them.

"Since it looks like we're never going to catch up with these guys," Wolff continued. "I've been thinking that I might just get me a little place down here, a thousand acres or so, run a few head of longhorns. Get me a beat up old pickin' up truck and learn to drink Lone Star beer out of long neck bottles."

"Shit," he laughed. "In just a few months, you won't be able to tell me from a native."

"You could do worse, *amigo,*" Cuervo said. "But if you're going to do that, you're going to have to get yourself the right kind of boots. You're never going to be a rancher wearing those black Wellingtons of yours. You've got to get some alligator skin cowboy boots."

Wolff laughed. "God knows, I don't want to wear the wrong boots."

"Not down here, you don't."

Dragon One Zero was the last of the four ships to arrive back at the base. And, since he had a ready audience, Wolff

103

made one of the hot landings he was famous for. Dropping down out of the sky at full throttle, he pulled maximum pitch at the last possible moment and flared out with the skids barely an inch or two above the tarmac.

"You're going to jam those skids up your ass doing that someday," Mugabe muttered.

"The day that happens," Wolff grinned as he chopped the throttles to the turbines. "They can gladly take my wings away because I'll have become too damned old and too slow to fly anyway."

Chapter 16

Bolen Air Base

The Tactical Operation Center was buzzing when Wolff, Mugabe and Cuervo walked in.

" 'Bout time you jokers got back," Buzz growled when he looked up from the comm screen and spotted them. "Wolff, you and Cuervo grab a cup of coffee and get into my office. We're having a staff meeting in zero two."

"Yes, sir."

"I guess it's time for my afternoon nap," Mugabe grinned as Wolff turned to go. "That's the advantage of my being a lowly gunner, I don't have to talk to the boss."

"Screw you," Wolff muttered as he walked off.

Inside the room, the two pilots found that Zumwald and Avilia were already waiting for the meeting. "What's up?" Wolff asked Zumwald.

The Tac Platoon leader shrugged. "I just got here myself. Probably more bum wadding from Washington."

Buzz walked into the room and closed the door behind

im. "We've finally got them," he said, triumphantly strid-
ig to his desk.

"The so-called 'Vengeance of God' has taken over the
egaplatform, that super oil rig some hundred and eighty
iles out into the Gulf. They took it over early this morning
nd they're threatening to blow it up if they aren't paid a
illion dollars."

"A billion dollars!" Wolff exploded. "Jesus!"

"That's what I thought too," Buzz said. "And," he con-
nued, "they're holding hostages."

"How many?" Zumwald, asked as he scribbled some
otes. "And do we know where they are being held?"

"The answer to both questions," Buzz replied, "is that
ve don't know anything. The local authorities are inter-
iewing the crewmen who were released and hope to get us
n accurate head count before too much longer."

"What's the drill this time?" Wolff asked. "The usual
errorists with hostages scenario? Jump in, kick ass and take
ames?"

"No," Buzz sighed. "No such luck. Unfortunately
Washington has declared that this will be another joint op-
ration cluster-fuck with the major emphasis on ending the
akeover without causing any damage to the platform.
Ve've got the Coast Guard, the Navy and the Air Force all
agerly waiting to lend us a helping hand."

"What, no Army involvement?" Zumwald asked sarcas-
ically. In the past, most of their joint operations had not
vorked all that well.

"Actually," Buzz replied. "The 82d Airborne is standing
by in case we need an airborne assault."

"Into the Gulf of Mexico?"

"Yup, that's what the Navy's job will be, fishing soggy
paratroopers out of the water."

Everyone in the room burst out laughing.

"So, what is our role in this joint operations plan?" Wolff
asked.

"Well," Buzz continued. "The powers that be have come

up with a plan to deliver the money peacefully tomorro
and then we're going to slam the door on those people on
they clear out of the platform.''

"But what if they don't feel like going along with th
scenario?'' Zumwald asked.

"Good question,'' Buzz agreed. "When, and if, th
happens I guess we'll just have to improvise. But for rig
now, we do not have permission from Washington to sho
up the most valuable collection of oil rigs in the world. An
I'm sorry to have to say that until further notice, Rules
Engagement Alpha are in effect.''

"Aw shit!'' Wolff groaned, shaking his head in di
gust. Rules of Engagement Alpha meant that the gunshi
pilots would have to get permission before they coul
use their weapons except in the case where a life was i
danger.

"My sentiments exactly,'' Buzz said. "But that's wha
Washington wants so that's how it has to be.'' He pause
and smiled. "At least for now.''

"When do we get to see what this place looks like?'' Wol
asked. No matter how good the plan was, he didn't want t
have to fly in blind, he at least needed to know what th
potential target looked like.

Buzz glanced over at the clock on the wall. "The reco
photos should be here in a couple more hours. We lucke
out for once this time. The Air Force had a K-12 satellit
just coming up on the horizon when we got the call an
they were able to maneuver it into position in time to tak
a couple of snaps for us.''

"So for now,'' Buzz continued. "Zoomie, I want you t
get your people ready. Wolfman, run a pre-mission chec
on your birds. And, Avilia, I want you to keep working o
the coordination with the other services. On an operatio
like this, I don't want any coordination screw-ups.''

The Dragon Flight commander looked at each of his me
in turn. "Any questions?''

Each man shook his head.

"Okay, that's all for now, I'll call you back in as soon as we get the recon photos."

Throughout the afternoon, the crews of Dragon Flight worked feverishly on their machines, getting them ready for the assault on the oil platform. There were ammunition loads to be checked, turbines to be fine-tuned, windscreens to be polished and a hundred and one other things that needed to be seen to. No one minded the work though, now that they had a real mission in the works and their days of driving endlessly around in the sky were over. And it was the kind of mission that they did best.

Even Gunner was whistling as he stood on the walkway on top of his ship's stub wings and popped open the turbine inspection panels. Jennings was always in a good mood when there was a good chance that he was going to get to pop caps on someone.

Daryl "Gunner" Jennings was the son of a Vietnam gunship pilot who had died late in the war. He had still been an infant when his father was killed in action. His mother later married another gunship pilot turned cop. As a boy, he had been raised on old chopper gunship war stories and grew up watching video copies of the classic Vietnam War movies.

A minor heart murmur had kept him out of military service, but it had not been bad enough to keep him from joining the TPF and graduating from the Griffin flight school. The Tac Force wasn't the military, but so far, duty with Dragon Flight had given him several opportunities to fire his chopper's guns in anger and he was always eager to do it again, hence his nickname.

As close as Dragon Flight duty was to being in the military, Gunner still dreamed of flying in a real combat environment and he was really looking forward to tomorrow's mission.

"Yo! Gunner!" Wolff called up to him. "You seen Cuervo anywhere around here?"

Jennings shook his head. "Not for the last half hour or

so.'' He didn't bother to tell Wolff that the last time he had seen him, the Mexican pilot had been talking to Sandra Revell again.

"If you see him, tell him that I want to go over the mission plan with him.''

"Right," Gunner said, snapping the inspection panel back in place and latching it securely down. When he did see Cuervo, maybe he could get his co-pilot back to help him get this bullshit maintenance check finished. "I'll keep a sharp eye out for him.''

A few hours later Lieutenant Zumwald stuck his head around the corner of the open door to Buzz's office. "You wanted to see me, sir?''

"Yeah," Buzz said glancing up from his computer monitor. The Dragon Flight commander looked tired. "Come on in, close the door and have a seat.''

"What's up sir?''

"Zoomie," Buzz sounded disgusted. "I'm afraid that your men are going to have to stand down for now.''

"But, sir," the Tac Platoon Leader protested. "What about the operation?''

"It's on hold for now.''

Zumwald leaned forward in his chair. "May I ask why, sir?'' he said formally.

"Well, it seems that there's a congressman from Texas who thinks that the Texas Rangers should have the honor of retaking the Megaplatform from the terrorists. We're out of the picture for now.''

"The honor?'' Zoomie snorted. "You're shitting me, sir. They didn't say that.''

"That's the way they look at things down here," Buzz said, shaking his head. "This is taking place off the shore of Texas and most of the companies who own the Megaplatform facilities are based in Texas, so they are claiming first whack at them.''

"Also, they scrapped the plan to pay the ransom first and

take care of them later. They're planning a full bore assault to recapture it.''

"Captain, the Texas Rangers are one of the best state law enforcement agencies in the nation," Zumwald admitted. "But I think this may be a little more than they are equipped to handle. I can't believe that they don't realize that this isn't a bunch of drug smugglers or wetbacks they're taking on this time. Those guys are real pros.''

"They've got all the information we have so they should know what they're going up against," Buzz replied.

"So what is the Tac Force supposed to do in the meantime, sir? Stand off to the side and lend them a hand when they step on their foreskins?''

"No," Buzz shook his head. "Not even that. The Rangers are going to go it alone with a little help from the Texas Air National Guard.''

"Jesus H. Christ!''

"That thought crossed my mind," Buzz said dryly.

"I thought that the reason that Congress created the Tac Force was to take care of threats like this, sir, rather than letting poorly equipped local forces get hurt when they step in it over their heads.''

"That was the idea," Buzz said quietly. "But remember, this is Texas. They've got their own ideas.''

"But, these mercenaries are somebody's private army.''

"I know," Buzz said. "But until we get further word, we are on stand down.''

"Yes, sir," Zumwald stood up, his expression was grim. "Is that all?''

"That's it for now, Zoomie. Stand 'em down, but don't let 'em get too far away. We may be back on this case before you know it.''

"You got it, sir.''

"And, Zoomie.''

"Sir.''

"Get that devious little mind of yours working on some way that we can take that place without blowing it out of the water.''

109

Zumwald grinned. "Yes sir."

"And," Buzz added. "Chase the Wolfman down for me will you? I want to give him the good news, too."

"He's going to love it."

Chapter 17

Bolen Air Base

With Dragon Flight on stand down while the Texas Rangers made their move, there was little for the chopper cops to do except to get caught up on the routine maintenance on their gunships. Red Larson held court on the flight line all morning, a new cigar clamped between his teeth as the crews of all four Griffins scurried around doing their best to look appropriately busy. If they didn't, they knew that Red would find something for them to do.

By noon, the four Griffins sparkled like new. Wolff and Mugabe had One Zero in tip top shape and were just finishing polishing the windscreen when Red walked up to them.

"You boys think you're done with this bird here?" he spoke around his cigar as his eyes swept the sleek lines of One Zero looking for anything that was not one hundred percent.

"Have a look," Wolff said, sweeping his arms wide to take in the entire ship from her wicked looking nose to her sharply raked tail fins. "She's spitshined and ready to uphold the honor of the Tac Force at a moment's notice. Any bad guys who get a look at this glistening machine will shit their pants and surrender immediately rather than do anything that will get her dirty."

"Wise ass," Red growled. "You think this is all a big fucking joke right?"

"No, I don't, Red," Wolff suddenly got serious. "But after all this time you ought to know that I keep my shit straight around here. We have less down time on this machine than any chopper in the entire TPF."

Red took the cigar from between his teeth and spat a soggy chunk of tobacco on the tarmac. "That's only because I'm always here to see that you two do your job."

"Fuck you, Red," Wolff said turning away.

Red got a puzzled look on his face, shrugged and walked off, wondering what was biting the Wolfman today.

"How 'bout some lunch," Mugabe said, glancing at his watch as he put the bottle of plexiglass polish and rag back in the lock box behind his seat.

"Suits me," Wolff said. "I've enjoyed about all of this 'make it look pretty' shit that I can stand for one morning."

"Shall we try the club again?"

"It's either that or risk dining at the gut wagon," the pilot said, referring to the snack van that made its rounds of the airbase three times a day.

"I came down here hoping for some down-home cookings," Mugabe shuddered. "Not some dried up buritto that's been baking under an infrared lamp since some time early yesterday morning."

Wolff laughed. "The club it is."

All small officers' clubs look the same. It doesn't matter which service runs them, they all have that same overly lighted, slightly tacky look that all federal officers come to know and love. The little club at Bolen Air Base was no exception to the rule, and the waitress on duty was a clone of a hundred other waitresses from Washington DC to Panama City. The two chopper cops felt right at home when they walked into the dining room.

"I don't like the idea of the Rangers trying to go it alone against those guys," Wolff said as he slid a chair out and sat down. "But it's about time that we had us a little break.

I wouldn't mind a couple of days off to wander around and see what the locals have to offer.''

"You know Buzz isn't going to let us get off the base,'' Mugabe said, waving a hand to get the waitress's attention. "Not until this thing is completely wrapped up.''

"Yeah,'' the pilot sighed. "But a man can dream can't he? Speaking of dreams,'' Wolff changed the subject. "You see Legs lately?''

Mugabe thought for a moment. "Now that you mention it, no. I wonder what she's been doing with herself on these sultry southern nights.?''

"Beats the shit outa me,'' Wolff laughed. "But she sure as hell ain't been doing it with me.''

"I think I just found out what Officer Sandra Revell's been doing,'' Mugabe said, lowering his voice as he looked over Wolff's shoulder toward the front door of the club.

Wolff turned around and saw Cuervo holding the door open for Legs. Sandra was smiling at something the Mexican officer was saying, her green eyes flashing. Wolff felt a jolt when he saw the look she gave her escort. He had never seen her look at any man that way before.

"Our man Arturo doesn't waste any time, does he?'' Mugabe said.

"I'll be a son of a bitch,'' Wolff said softly, trying hard to keep his voice neutral. "It looks like he's got her number for sure.''

"That it does,'' Mugabe agreed.

"Any time ya'll are ready,'' the bleached blonde waitress said, snapping her wad of gum impatiently. "I'll take your orders.''

"Ah,'' Wolff fumbled with the menu. He had been so focused on Legs that he hadn't seen her approach their table. "I'll have a BLT and a draft.''

Mugabe ordered the same and went back to watching Wolff watch Legs. He had never seen the Wolfman lose his cool this way before. Wolff definitely liked the ladies and he had his normal ups and downs with them like any man. But whatever happened, the Wolfman always kept his cool. That was part of his charm and one of the biggest reasons that women found him so attractive, he never got over-anxious and he was never jealous.

Mugabe knew that his partner had more than a casual interest in the tall blonde chopper cop. The flirtatious edge to the bickering and biting that went on between those two was obvious to everyone. There was even a pool among the maintenance crew to see when the Wolfman would finally get her in the sack and Mugabe had twenty dollars down saying that it would be before the end of the year.

It looked now, however, that all bets were off.

"Hey, if you're not going to eat your fries," Mugabe asked. "Can I have them before they get cold?"

"Sure," Wolff said, pushing his plate across the table, never taking his eyes off Sandra.

Revell was so engrossed in her conversation with Arturo that she didn't notice that Wolff couldn't take his eyes off her. But finally she glanced over at his table and saw that he was staring at her with a very strange expression on his face. She briefly wondered what in the hell was wrong with him, before she turned her smiling green eyes and full attention back to Arturo. She was enjoying herself too much to let anything interfere with it.

The first day that Sandra had showed up for duty at Dragon Flight, a smiling Rick Wolff had sauntered up to her and asked her for a date. Trying to make a good first impression, she had patiently explained that she didn't date the men she worked with.

"Great," he had laughed. "Since you're not flying with me, we can have dinner tonight."

She had been sorely tempted by Wolff's boyish good looks, his deep green eyes and his easy smile, but she went on to explain to him that she was serious about not dating in the force. He had just smiled, slowly running his green eyes up and down her frame.

"Okay, Legs," he had said. "I'll catch you later on the flight line."

The nickname had stuck and so had her determination

not to go out with him. It had become a ritual with them, every couple of weeks he would ask her for a date and every time she would turn him down. Sandra's rigid rule about not dating the men she worked with was her insurance that she wouldn't be taken for just another thrill-seeking bimbo playing games in a man's job. And, even though under other circumstances, she probably would have fallen for the dashing pilot's line, she made no exceptions, not even for the Wolfman.

Sandra Revell had worked hard to get where she was and she wasn't about to take any shit from anyone, on or off the force, about being a woman cop. She had never turned down an assignment, no matter how tough, and she had never complained when the men tried to make her lose her temper or quit. Anytime she got any shit from one of the men, she just waited patiently until the next hand-to-hand class and then proceeded to kick his ass up between his ears.

As a result, Sandra Revell was well respected around Dragon Flight and most of the men she worked with seemed to have forgotten that she was a woman. Some of the rest of them, however, stung by her refusal to play their macho games had started a rumor that she was a lesbian. She really didn't give a shit what they thought, but she had to admit that her love life hadn't been that great lately. Too many of the men she dated had figured her for an easy screw just because she was a woman cop.

Sandra laughed at something Arturo said, her clear voice ringing across the small dining room.

"Come on", Wolff growled, shooting a last look her way. "Let's get out of this fucking dump."

"Sure thing, partner."

Later that afternoon, Wolff and Mugabe were hanging out by the soft drink machine in the shade of the hangar when they spotted Gunner Jennings wandering by. He changed course when he saw the two and sauntered up to the drink cooler. Plugging in his Unicard, he dialed up an RC Cola, popped the top and took a long drink.

"I can't believe how fucking hot it can be in November down here."

"Beats freezing your ass off in the Mile High City," Mugabe replied.

"But at least I could go skiing."

"I haven't seen Legs around this afternoon," Wolff said casually.

"She's running that Mexican pilot through the turret weapons simulator," Gunner answered with a grin. "Region wants us to give him as much hands-on time with the Griffin as we can to give him a head start on the conversion program."

"Sure he's not doing hands-on time with Legs instead?" Mugabe grinned.

"She has been spending a lot of time with him the last couple of days," Gunner admitted with a shrug. "But she's a big girl." Jennings had long ago quit trying to make time with his beautiful co-pilot or even take any interest in what she did on her off-duty time.

"In fact," he continued, taking another swig from his cola. "She's been walking around with her head up her ass ever since that guy showed up. I've had to get on her case a couple of times lately to get her mind back on her business."

That was not what Wolff had wanted to hear at all. "I'm getting tired of sitting around on my ass all day," he suddenly growled.

"I thought you wanted some time off?" Mugabe smiled.

"I changed my mind," Wolff snapped back. "That all right with you?"

"Sure, buddy," Mugabe held up his hands, "Anything you say." The gunner knew his pilot's moods and this was one of those times when it was easiest to just go along with whatever the Wolfman wanted to do.

"Since we aren't on ramp alert tonight, you want to see if we can get permission to go off base?" Mugabe asked. "Maybe grab some of that Tex-Mex food I've been hearing about and a couple of beers while we check out the local talent?''

"Sure," Wolff said, without much enthusiasm as his eyes swept past the officers' club. "It beats the shit outa hanging around this fucking place again tonight."

Chapter 18

The Megaplatform

Travis Cunningham III leaned back and put his silver-tipped, ostrich-skin cowboy boots up on the desk in the control room at the central platform and watched as the sun dropped down over the horizon of the Gulf of Mexico. So far, his operation was going exactly the way he had planned it, to the letter.

He smiled to himself and lit another cigarette. By this time tomorrow, he'd be a multi-millionaire and the day after that, he'd be lying on the beach in Rio with a cold drink in one hand and a dark skinned beauty wearing one of those skimpy, string bikinis in the other. He sighed. Not too bad for less than a week's work.

Someone knocked on the door to the control room breaking his reverie.

"Come in," Cunningham said, turning away from the view of the Megaplatform below.

"We need to talk," Falcon said, striding into the room. His face was hard and his eyes cold.

"What about?"

"The exchange tomorrow," the Arab looked concerned. "I don't like it."

"What's not to like?" Cunningham asked with a shrug. "They give us a billion dollars, we give them half of the

116

hostages and then we all disappear into the sunset rich men. What's wrong with that?"

"It's been just too easy," Falcon said thoughtfully, looking down at the platform below. "They're planning something. I'm certain of it."

"Like what?"

The Arab looked back at the oilman and shrugged. "How do you say it? A double cross?"

Cunningham sat back in his chair. "They won't try to fuck with me on this," he said quietly, looking out over the complex. "Not if they're smart. I'm in complete control of the world's biggest offshore oil rig and they fucking well know it. One snap of my fingers and this all gets turned into expensive junk."

Falcon shrugged again. "I know all of that, any idiot would, but I still have a bad feeling about the exchange. I would feel better about it if you had set it up for a credit transfer to a Swiss bank. That way we wouldn't have to let them inside our defenses."

"I like the feel of long green," Cunningham said. "Plus, the fucking Swiss have gotten real selfrighteous about who puts what in their banks lately." He did not mention to the Arab that in his haste, he had not even thought of handling it that way. He had always been more comfortable with cold cash in his hand.

"Regardless, I plan to have the men on full alert tomorrow," Falcon said.

"What can they do?"

"They can bring in the Tac Force."

"They can shit too, if they eat enough," Cunningham snorted. "If I see even one of those hotshot choppers of theirs in the sky, I'll blow that holding tank as sure as shit stinks."

Cunningham's ransom message had contained a warning that if any attempt was made to re-take the Megaplatform before he was paid, he would release the millions of gallons of oil in the big holding tank and contaminate the Gulf shore from Pensacola to Brownsville. After the problems the

Exxon Valdez spill had caused in Alaska, no one was willing to risk killing the richest fishing grounds in the United States over a measly billion dollars.

"Nonetheless," the Arab said. "I am taking no chances tomorrow."

"Do what you like," Cunningham said, his voice taking on a sharp tone. "But don't fuck up the exchange. Remember, some of that money's yours too."

"I haven't forgotten," Falcon said. "Neither have the men."

"It's your job to see that they don't."

Falcon walked out and closed the door behind him, leaving Cunningham to his dreams of wealth.

The Arab hurried on down to the dayroom that had been taken over by the mercenaries as a headquarters. When he walked in, he saw Captain Geoffery De Lancy, late of his Majesty's Grenadier Guards Regiment, pouring dark Jamaican rum into a canteen cup half full of coffee.

"We need to talk," he said.

"I say, old man, what's wrong?" the mercenary captain, asked, taking a healthy slug of the coffee and rum mixture. "Troubles with the fat Yank again?"

The Arab took a glass from the counter, rinsed it and reached for De Lancy's bottle.

"I thought that you people didn't indulge," the officer said sarcastically.

"Allah will forgive me for this," Falcon said, pouring a stiff double shot of the dark rum. "He knows that I am a fool and the son of a fool." He knocked back the rum and poured another.

"Steady on, old man," De Lancy said nervously. "That has to last me 'till I get to one of the islands. Now, what seems to be the problem?" De Lancy was all business now. He might have gotten cashiered from his regiment for bottle problems, but money had always come first with him. Any talk of this operation not working out as planned had his fullest attention.

"I fear that Mister Cunningham is not taking this situation seriously enough."

"And exactly how is that?" De Lancy asked. His fondness for rum aside, De Lancy had a first class military mind which was the one and only reason that he was commanding Falcon's mercenary troops. The Arab had not survived as long as he had in the mercenary world by picking incompetent drunks to work for him.

"He's overestimating the power he has," Falcon said. "And, at the same time, he's seriously underestimating our opposition."

"Not good," De Lancy said, taking a small sip of his rum laden coffee. "Perhaps we need to keep a closer eye on our employer. The lads and I would hate to miss a payday just because of him."

"That's exactly what I was thinking."

"Just what did you have in mind?" the Brit asked, setting his cup down.

"I want everyone on full alert tomorrow," Falcon said. "In case they get the idea to deliver us something more than the ransom money. I want the missile men in place and ready to fire at the first sign of trouble."

The mercenaries were well equipped with the Israeli-made, Bee Sting II anti-aircraft missiles. While not quite as potent as the new American Viper missiles, the shoulder-fired, infrared guided Bee Stings would be able to take care of anything sent against them.

"We can do that easily enough," De Lancy said. "As the Yanks say, 'No Sweat.'"

"Good," Falcon still looked grim. "I don't want any slipups tomorrow."

119

Chapter 19

"Good morning, *amigos*, Cuervo sounded cheerful, as he sauntered up to Wolff and Mugabe. "It's a beautiful day for flying, no?"

When Wolff didn't respond and looked down at the ground, the Mexican pilot's smile faded. "What is wrong, my friends?" he asked.

"Just leave it alone," Mugabe tried to warn him.

At that moment Legs walked up to her ship and Cuervo caught the look on Wolff's face when he spotted her. Instantly, he knew what the problem was.

"Wolff, I'm very sorry," he said, reaching out to take the pilot's arm. "I didn't know that she was your woman. If I had known I would not have . . ."

Wolff shrugged out of his reach, his face set. "Just one thing, *amigo*." His voice was cold and even. "She is not my woman. Officer Revell is her own woman, both on and off-duty. What she does with her time is her own affair and no one else's. Got that?"

"I see," Cuervo said, backing away from the pilot. He knew that he was treading on very dangerous ground. "As I said, I didn't know . . ."

"That's what you said," Wolff snapped, taking half a step forward. "Let's just leave it at that, okay?"

Mugabe laid his hand on Cuervo's shoulder. "Let's go get a cup of coffee," he said, drawing the Mexican flyer away from Wolff. "We still have some time before the patrol briefing." Even though the Texas Rangers were going to make the assault on the Megaplatform alone today, Buzz had still scheduled a patrol just in case all of the terrorists weren't on the platform.

"Ah, sure, Mojo," Cuervo said, grateful for a way to gracefully get out of this situation. "I could sure use another cup."

Wolff watched Mugabe lead Cuervo away and fought to calm himself. Deep inside, he knew that it wasn't Cuervo's fault, any man with a pair of balls would try to connect with Sandra. And, if she responded, that was her business. He kept telling himself that over and over again.

"Grow up, asshole," he snarled at himself. "You fucking never had anything going with her anyway, so forget it."

Wolff said it, he didn't believe it. If nothing else, he had counted on the fact that he worked with her every day to finally do the trick. He had never thought that something like this would happen. That an outsider would cut in on him.

Texas Ranger Captain John Wayne Zimmermann looked out across the row of Texas National Guard choppers sitting on the tarmac at National Guard air base and shook his head. Zimmermann had been a Ranger all of his adult life, just as his father had been and his father before him all the way back to the days before the Texas Republic. He had served the Lone Star state to the very best of his abilities for over twenty years and for the first time in a long, distinguished career, he was seriously considering refusing to obey his orders.

He wasn't afraid of a dangerous mission. He had faced danger hundreds of times in his career, it was just part of wearing the star. But this time he was afraid that a mistake was being made, a serious mistake, and there was a damned politician behind it. Zimmermann was a lawman to his bones and he had learned to distrust politicians as a matter of principle. Little good ever came from a politician sticking his nose into law enforcement matters.

Like any good cop, Zimmermann knew his limitations as

well as the limitations of the force he commanded. The Texas Rangers were the best there were when it came to what they did. But, he knew that they were a state police force, not a tactical assault force. He had read the after action reports and the prisoner interrogation sheets from the Federal Tac Force and he knew that they were going up against real professionals. He knew that his boys would do their best, they always did their best or they wouldn't be Rangers, but he also knew that some of his people were going to die today.

He glanced down at his watch, five minutes to go. He hitched his pants up over his lanky hips and settled his gun belt over the bottom of his flak jacket. Damnit anyway, it was time to go and no Zimmermann since his great, great grandfather had ever turned his back on a fight. He looked over at the Rangers lounging in the shade of the hangar.

"Okay boys," he called out. "Ya'll get your gear and climb on board."

Five minutes later, the five National Guard UH-1N Hueys and their two AH-1S Cobra gunship escorts lifted off the helipad and turned south for the Gulf of Mexico. In a little over an hour, they would arrive at the Megaplatform and write another chapter in the long history of the Texas Rangers. He hoped the chapter would have a happy ending.

By the time Wolff walked into the TOC for the briefing, he had himself under tight control. After all, he was the unflappable Wolfman and he had a hard-earned reputation to uphold. He caught Cuervo's eye and nodded in an unspoken apology between two men. Cuervo nodded back in an unspoken acceptance. They would continue to fly together, but they would never be friends again.

Wolff was busy looking at his inflight checklist when Legs walked into the room with Gunner, and he kept his eyes glued to his clipboard.

"Fuck it," he thought, refusing to accept any more juvenile self-pity and turned his attention back to the briefing.

122

"Okay people," Buzz said. "As you all know, the Texas Rangers are going to try to re-take the oil rig this morning. Supposedly, all of the terrorists are there, but I'm not taking any chances, I'm sending One Three up to patrol the coastline offshore just in case. I want the rest of you standing by in flight gear in case we're needed.

His eyes swept the room, "Any questions?"

There were none. "Okay, get to it."

Wolff walked past Legs on his way to his locker to get into his flight gear, but she didn't see him. She was looking across the room at Cuervo. The pilot quickly dressed and walked out onto the flight line. The winter sun was bright in the clear blue sky and a breeze was blowing in from the Gulf. This was pretty country, but Wolff didn't think that he'd ever want to come back to Texas.

"How about a cup of coffee?" Red asked, walking up to the pilot.

"You trying to poison me?" Wolff said attempting to make a joke.

"Just thought that you might like a cup," Red said gruffly, "But, if you don't . . ."

"Okay," the pilot said. "I'll risk poisoning." Red's coffee was famous in Dragon Flight. Most of the chopper cops thought that it should be reclassified as a controlled substance, but they were always ready to have a cup when they needed a quick eye opener.

Red's office away from home looked exactly like his office back at their Denver home base, cluttered beyond belief. Wolff walked over to the pot that was perched on the top of a bulging filing cabinet, grabbed a convenient dirty cup and filled it with the evil brew.

He cautiously took a sip and sat down in the only empty chair. "It's a little weak today, Red. What's the matter, you run out of battery acid?"

"Wise ass."

Red poured himself a cup and the two men started talking about the Rangers' mission. Both of them agreed that it was a shame that once more local politics had gotten the better of what should have been a purely tactical decision. But they had both seen this happen time and time again, it was a fact of life in police work.

"Well," Wolff said getting to his feet, "It's time, I'd better go see how the Rangers do."

"You take care now," Red said in a rare, honest show of concern.

"Yeah."

As the scheduled time for the Rangers' assault approached, Buzz had one of the radios in the TOC tuned to the Rangers' radio frequency. Most of the chopper cops had crowded into the TOC, waiting to listen to the assault. None of them wished the Rangers any bad luck, but they all knew that they should be making the attack instead of an overly brave, but ill-equipped state police force like the Texas Rangers.

They could hear the Texas pilots talking to one another as they flew over the Gulf of Mexico. Their flight leader, Lone Star Six, was the National Guard pilot piloting one of the Cobra gunships.

"Lone Star Five, this is Six," he radioed to his wingman as they approached the huge oil platform. "I'm going on down to take a look now. You keep the slicks back there with you, over."

"This is Star Five," the other gunship pilot radioed back. "Roger, Six. Ya'll be careful now, you hear."

"This is Lone Star Six," the flight leader answered. "Rolling in now."

"Five this is Six," he came back on the air a moment later. "It looks pretty good so far. I don't see . . ."

"Lock on! Lock on!" someone suddenly yelled over the radio, breaking into Six's transmission.

"Five, this is Six, They've got . . ." there was silence on the frequency.

There was a brief pause and someone else came on the air. "Oh Jesus! Six! Six!"

There was no answer.

"Lone Star Flight, this is Five," the wingman radioed. The panic in his voice was apparent. "Six is down! Break for home! They've got missiles!"

The channel was suddenly filled with panicked voices of the Huey pilots as they frantically tried to get their slow, unarmed ships out of danger. Most of them made it. Only one Huey, the one carrying Ranger Captain Zimmermann, took a hit. It fell from the sky a blazing wreck and crashed into the Gulf a mile from the platform.

"Shit!" Wolff muttered as he listened to the other pilots report that they could not see any survivors. Everyone on board the doomed ship had died in the fiery explosion.

"Poor bastards," Zumwald said softly.

"I want you in my office now," Buzz announced gravely to his staff. "We've got work to do."

The chopper cops were stunned and silent as they filed in to plan their next move. Suddenly, the blue skies over the Gulf of Mexico weren't as friendly as they had been just a few moments before.

Texas Ranger John Wayne Zimmermann was the fifth in an unbroken line of Zimmermanns to wear a lawman's star for the state of Texas, and he was the second Zimmermann to die upholding the laws of his state.

Later that afternoon, when the bodies were recovered by the Coast Guard, the captain's oldest son, Ranger Sergeant Fred Zimmermann flew his father's body back to the north Texas town of Fredrichsburg for burial in the family plot. Rather than staying around for the funeral, he flew back to Austin the same evening and requested that he be assigned to work with the Federal Tac Force until the terrorists holding the Megaplatform were eliminated.

His request was granted.

Chapter 20

The Megaplatform

The Rangers' attack on the Megaplatform had jarred Travis Cunningham III out of his smug complacency and sent him into a blind rage. Falcon had been right, the bastards weren't going to play fair. They had planned to kill him instead of giving him the money they owed him.

As far as he was concerned, the ransom money was owed to him and he wasn't going to let anything get in the road of his getting it. And, by God, he was going to show them that he wasn't fucking around. He'd show those bastards that Travis Cunningham III was every bit as good a man as his grandfather had been. When he said that he would do something, then by God he would.

He stormed down out of the control tower and raced across the platform to the valve control unit for the oil holding tanks. Like everything else at the Megaplatform, the transfer tanks were electronically controlled, but he had already taken the precaution of jamming the safety switch in the open position.

"Fuck with me, will you?" Cunningham snarled to no one, "I'll show you bastards."

With the flick of a switch, he quickly opened the dump valves and activated the pumps. Thick black crude oil started gushing out of the huge pipes and quickly formed an enormous inky black blot on the Gulf's surface. In minutes, the oil slick was drifting with the tide, heading for the coast of Texas a hundred and eighty miles away.

From the rail by the helipad, Falcon watched the oil pour out onto the water and slowly shook his head. He knew how

Americans felt about the environment. There was really going to be hell to pay for this. He turned and went down below decks to find De Lancy.

A half a million gallons of crude oil later, Cunningham shut off the pumps and headed back up to the central control room. Closing the door behind him, the oilman activated the modem on the computer and pulled out the keyboard. Eagle might be tied up, brown-nosing with those damned Tac Force cops, but he needed to talk to him anyway. He desperately needed advance warning of what those bastards were going to try to do to him next.

He quickly typed a phone number as soon as the screen came alive.

The screen displayed the word, "Dialing." The word blinked off and on as the computer rang the number.

"Fuck," Cunningham shouted, pounding his fist on the table. "Where is that Goddamned wetback?"

The screen continued to blink its message, "Dialing."

A frustrated Cunningham was just about to shut the system down when the dialing message stopped blinking and the words, "Go ahead" appeared on the screen.

"This is Mister Smith," he typed.

"What kind of Smith?"

"Condor"

"This is Eagle, go ahead."

Falcon found De Lancy in their temporary headquarters in the dayroom. "We need to talk," he told the mercenary leader.

"About what?" De Lancy asked.

"About rethinking this entire operation."

"What's on your mind?"

"Cunningham," Falcon said simply. "He's out of control."

De Lancy happened to agree. But, as it happened all too many times in mercenary operations, once you were committed, even to work for a madman, it was very difficult to find an easy way to back out. Not only did it put a sizeable dent in your pay check, it could also hurt your reputation and your chances for future work.

A mercenary lived on his reputation and his scoreboard did not just record his battles won and lost. It also recorded how loyal he was to his employer. De Lancy had never broken a contract yet, but this was beginning to appear as if he should take another very careful look at this particular situation. He also knew that whatever he did, if he managed to get out of this one alive, he would never take another contract to operate on water. If they were on land, he would stand a chance of getting away if things went bad. But, where he was, a hundred and eighty miles out in the middle of the Gulf of Mexico, it was a long swim to safety.

"What are you thinking about doing?" he asked, a trace of anxiety in his voice.

"As far as I'm concerned," the Arab said, "Cunningham is in violation of our contract."

Falcon did not make that statement lightly. He had been in the mercenary business for many years, first as a fighter and then as a principal, the man who brought units together for potential employers. He too stood to lose a lot if he abandoned Cunningham, more perhaps than De Lancy.

The mercenary captain had worked with Falcon several times before and knew his reputation as being the best in the business. If he thought that they were supporting a lost cause, De Lancy was going to listen. "Go on."

"Our contract did not include trying to hold this oil rig against the Tac Force. Even knowing when they are coming does not guarantee us a fighting chance against them. If nothing else, they can just starve us out."

"But the oil holding tanks, do you think they will risk greater pollution in the Gulf?"

"I think that what Cunningham has already done is going to make them furious and screaming for our blood," Falcon answered. "As of right now, though, I think they will worry about that after they have sent the Tac Force

128

after us. And, from everything I know about the Tac Force, they won't let a little thing like pollution get in their way."

"So, what's your plan?"

"I'm going to call one of the hydrofoils over here and start using it for our operations center. That way, if it does go bad, we can try to make a run for it. I've been in communication with our contact in the Cayman Islands. He says that he can get us out of the country if we can reach him."

"What's to keep the Tac Force from blowing us out of the water if we make a run for it?"

"Your missiles and a few hostages."

De Lancy made his mind up fast. "Count me in," he said. "But what about the men?"

"That is a problem." Falcon agreed. One inviolate part of the unwritten mercenary's code was that you never left your men behind, dead or alive. A mercenary always fought harder knowing that he would go home after the operation one way or the other. "I don't see any way that we can get all of them into the boat, it's not that big."

"That's going to cause problems," De Lancy said. "They're not going to be pleased when they see that they're being left behind."

"That's a discipline problem," Falcon said. "And I believe that troop discipline is your department."

De Lancy looked at the Arab for a moment. "I do want to take my cadre with us," he said quietly. "They've been with me for a long time."

"No more than six men," Falcon said. "Alert them and tell them to be ready to leave on a moment's notice."

"Six it is," De Lancy answered, thinking of the rest of his men. "Poor bastards."

It wasn't until noon of the next day that the control of the Megaplatform recovery operation was officially turned back over to Buzz and his Dragon Flight Chopper cops. The Texas congressman who had insisted that the Rangers have the honor of retaking the platform had to be run down first and convinced that a hell of lot more than the honor of the Lone Star state was at stake now.

The massive oil slick that had been released was rapidly approaching the richest fishing grounds in the Gulf Coast region and a national disaster of catastrophic proportions was in the making. The EPA already had every available cleanup ship on station trying to contain the slick and any further release of oil would overwhelm their ability to control it.

Once more, Buzz and the Tac Force were on the hot seat. One half of Washington was screaming that the Megaplatform had to be retaken immediately while the other half was screaming that the Tac Force had better not do anything that would create more oil pollution. But as always, it was easy to order a thing done, an entirely different matter, however, to do it. And this time, the Tac Force was really walking a tightrope.

The word had also been passed down that the federal antiterrorists statutes had been invoked, making only one solution to the problem possible. Under no circumstances would a ransom be paid and the Tac Force was not authorized to negotiate with the terrorists. Either the terrorists would surrender, or the platform would be retaken by force. Since there was no indication that Cunningham was going to call it quits, brute force was the only option left.

In the TOC, Buzz and his staff were preparing their plans again. This time, however, ROE Charlie was in effect, the shoot on sight order and they were planning accordingly. This time, a representative from the Texas Rangers was sitting in on the meeting in case there was anything their forces could contribute to the operation.

They were going over the Air Force satellite photographs of the Megaplatform millimeter by millimeter looking for anything that would give them a clue as to what the terrorists had done to defend the platform.

"I can't see much," Zumwald said. "Except that some

130

makeshift barricades have been thrown up around the central platform."

"That and the obstacles they've planted in the middle of all of the helipads," Wolff added.

"That's no problem for us," Zumwald said. "We can always rappel down."

"And get your shit blown away while you're doing it," Wolff said. "Remember these guys aren't your typical drug maggot types who are going to panic when we show up, they're real pros. They're disciplined and they're well armed with automatic weapons and surface to air missiles."

"Okay," Buzz said. "Let's get down to the nuts and bolts. "Zoomie, what have you come up with?"

"Well sir." the Tac Platoon Leader said looking down at his notes. "From what I have right now, it looks like we'll be facing thirty to forty of Cunningham's mercenaries and it has been confirmed that they have four armed helicopters supporting them along with anti-aircraft missiles and automatic weapons. The way I see it, we have two separate tactical problems here. One is that the terrorists are holding hostages and the other one is they're in control of all that oil. If I read the situation right, Washington is far more concerned about preventing further oil contamination than they are about the people being held hostage."

"That's about it," Buzz admitted.

"In that case, sir," Zumwald tapped the recon photo of the oil containment facility. "I recommend that we try to take the oil away from them first and then worry about the hostage situation later."

Buzz thought for a moment. "How do you want to do that?"

"Well, considering the missiles and everything, I was thinking about doing a Halo parachute drop."

"What in the hell is that?"

"A High Altitude, Low Opening jump, sir," Zumwald grinned. "We exit the aircraft at 10,000 feet or so, free fall to the target and open our chutes at 500 feet."

"And die," Wolff added dryly.

131

"No," Zumwald said. "It's easy. Remember when I got to take the platoon through that Army Ranger training program? Well anyway, we all did a night Halo drop and a day jump should be a piece of cake."

"But no one was shooting at you on the way down," Wolff reminded him. "This jump isn't going to be any Mickey Mouse training exercise."

"But that's where you come in," Zumwald told the pilot with a smile. "If your gunships can keep their heads down for the thirty seconds it takes for us to hit the platform after the chutes deploy, we should be able to make it, no sweat. With the steerable chutes, we can land anywhere on the platform within a meter of where we want to be."

Buzz looked thoughtful. "And then what?"

"Once we're down, we secure the pumps and the oil tanks and then sit tight until the rest of you can get the situation under control."

"It's risky," Buzz said. "But it has a certain logic to it. How many men do you want to use and where are you going to get the Halo equipment?"

"I'll need six men. Myself and one of the Tac Teams."

Buzz raised an eyebrow. "Won't you be needed with the rest of your platoon?"

"My Platoon Sergeant Garcia can take care of the rest of the operation, sir," Zumwald said firmly. "I think it's best that I be with the jumpers."

"And the equipment?"

"I can borrow it from the Army Rangers at Fort Bragg. I've got a friend there who can have it here first thing tomorrow morning."

"How do you want to go in?" Buzz asked. "In one of the Griffins or do you want Avilia to round up some Air Force transport for you?"

"I'd rather ride with one of our own ships, sir. It gives me a little more control of the operation."

"You can go with me," Wolff said.

"Okay," Buzz said. "Let's do it. Now, how do you intend to reduce the rest of their positions?"

132

"After we've secured the oil, I'd like to start with the central control platform. With a little bit of help from the Griffins we can get the rest of the platoon down, secure it and then work our way from there through the rest of them one at a time."

He glanced down at his notes. "What is it? Fourteen platforms in all?"

"Right."

"One thing I will need is backup from the Texas Rangers to occupy the platforms after we clear them and take custody of the prisoners for us."

"That can be easily arranged," the Ranger representative spoke up for the first time. "We'll be glad to get our hands on those guys. We owe them one."

Chapter 21

Bolen Air Base

"Okay Wolff," Buzz said, turning to the Dragon Flight leader. "Your turn, what's the air support plan?"

"First," Wolff said. "I'd like to go back to those missiles that nailed the Rangers' chopper. Has anyone been able to get a firm ID on them yet?"

Buzz shook his head. "All we know is that they seemed to be heat seekers. The Rangers don't have the sensors we have to pick up on that kind of thing and they were all just a little too busy trying to save their asses to take notes on what went flying past them"

"I can appreciate that," the pilot said. "But it gives us a bit of an edge if we know what they're likely to be shooting at us."

"You'll just have to plan for the worst," Buzz said.

"I'll have Red install the Black Hole IR suppression kits on the birds and make sure that the decoy flare launchers are loaded."

"No problem there," Buzz agreed. "Then what?"

"Well sir," Wolff continued. "If these guys are on the ball at all, and we have every reason to think that they will be, they'll have at least one of their choppers in the air to give them early warning of anything coming their way. That and the air traffic control radar in the tower will make it damned difficult for us to achieve any kind of surprise attack, so we've got to overwhelm them quickly."

"How are you planning to do that?"

"First off, I'll be using two ships to carry the Tac Platoon and the other two as fire support gunships. As I said, I'll take Zoomie's Halo team with me, but after they're airborne, I'll lead the fire support team."

"Now I would like to have surveillance aircraft stationed at ten to fifteen thousand feet over that platform at all times until the assault. High enough that they stay out of range of the missiles, but low enough that they will be picked up on the control tower radar."

"I want them to think that we're maintaining a close watch on them," he explained. "Then, when the time for the assault comes, I will replace the high cover with my Griffin while the other three choppers are moving in down at wave top level under the radar.

"After offloading Zoomie and his team, I'll drop out of the sky and take out their early warning bird while Zoomie's people are free falling. Then, as soon as I drop that bird, I'll make a strafing run over the platform right as the Tac Team is popping their chutes."

"That's going to be tight," Buzz looked concerned. "Maybe a little too tight."

"I know," Wolff nodded. "But I don't see how else we're going to do it. The way they're armed, we can't do our normal fire suppression runs without having to dodge missiles."

Buzz had to agree. "Okay, what happens after Zoomie has taken control of the oil tanks?"

"We just call 'em up and tell 'em that it's all over." Wolff shrugged.

"There's still the hostages," Buzz reminded him. "Don't forget that."

"But we have our standing orders about hostage situations," Zumwald broke in. "The hostages won't be of any real use to them."

"There's still a lot of people who aren't familiar with the provisions of the Counter Terrorist Act," Buzz reminded them. "You'll have to make them believe that we will fire even if the hostages are in the way."

"We'll tell them," Wolff said. "But if they decide not to give themselves up, the other fire support ship and I will clear that big platform so the troop carriers can set down. First off, however, we'll team up and try to take out the guys with the missiles. A little double whammy and get them to fire them all at us."

"Isn't that a bit risky?"

"Not as risky as letting them get a lock on one of the troop carriers," Wolff answered with a shrug. "Then, once the first platform is cleared, we'll just keep clearing them one at a time until all of them are dead or they give up."

"You make it sound simple," Buzz said.

"It's going to be a gold-plated bitch," Wolff admitted. "But I don't see any other way to do it."

Buzz asked if there was anything else to discuss but there was nothing. "Well, gentlemen," he said. "I guess that's it for now, I want you to brief your people and get ready. I'll be briefing the other services on our plan, so Wolff, Zumwald, I want you two to keep close by so I can find you in a hurry in case any glitches turn up that we have to get nailed down."

"Yes, sir," both men answered.

"Make sure that you get all the loose ends tied down

tonight, gentlemen," Buzz said. "There won't be any time tomorrow for fuckups."

While Buzz and his staff hashed out the details of the operation, Red's people were out on the flight line slaving over the four Griffins, getting them ready for the mission in the morning. Red paced back and forth, chomping on his dead cigar and trying to be everywhere at once. Even at the best of times, Red Larson tended to over-supervise his crew, but at times like this, he really cracked the whip over them.

He walked over to the two men installing the eighteen round 2.75 inch rocket pods under the stub wings of Dragon One Zero. "Listen, numb nuts," he growled at the ordnance technician struggling with the attachment bolts. "You tighten the sway braces after you have secured the main attachment bolts. Got that?"

"Yes, sir," the man said. "It's just that . . ."

"I don't want to fucking hear it," Red shot back. "You do it by the fucking numbers or I will kick your fucking ass. Got it?"

"Yes, sir."

"Jesus," the other ordnance man muttered once the maintenance chief was safely out of ear shot, "What's biting Red's ass today?"

"He gets bad before assault jobs," the first man said. "But how'd you like to go get me another bolt for this fucker. The threads are galled on this one."

"Sure thing," the second man said, glad to get off the flight line and out of Red's sight for even a few minutes.

"And don't take all fucking day about it."

"Right."

Down the flight line, Red glanced over and saw a mechanic lay a pair of pliers on top of the IR sensor housing. "Yo!" he yelled. "You! Dick head!"

The mechanic looked up.

"Get those fucking pliers off the fucking sensor before you find them stuck up your fucking nose!"

136

Red glared while the mechanic hastily stuck the pliers in his pocket. What was wrong with his people today? Didn't they know this was important?

As soon as Jack Zumwald finished picking his Halo team and had briefed his platoon, he went to his room to take care of his own personal mission preparations. He started by giving his 9mm Heckler and Koch MP-5 assault rifle a thorough cleaning. As an officer and the leader of the Tactical Platoon, he could have had the unit armorer clean his weapons for him, but that was the one thing he never trusted to anyone else. In his line of work, his weapons were his life and if a fuckup cost him his life, he wanted it to be his own fuckup, not someone else's.

The routine work calmed his mind. The soothing, familiar motions were part of Zumwald's mental preparation for combat and helped him get over his pre-mission jitters. He had discovered that the more apprehensive he was about a mission, the more time he spent getting ready for it. As he worked, the platoon leader realized that he was unconsciously very uneasy about the mission tomorrow when he found himself disassembling his MP-5 magazines and checking the spring tension on each and every one.

He didn't have to be a military genius to know why he was feeling uneasy about this mission. Making a daylight Halo drop onto a defended position and then taking it away from a band of professional mercenaries was not going to be a walk through the park. No matter what, someone was going to get killed tomorrow.

Zumwald forced his mind back to his preparations and reassembled his magazines. Then he carefully wiped any speck of dirt off every round of 9mm ammunition before reloading them. When each magazine was reloaded, he tapped the back side of it against the sole of his boot to seat the base of the rounds against the back wall of the magazine. Only then did he put them back into his ammo pouches.

Next, the lieutenant stripped his 10mm Glock pistol,

thoroughly cleaned it and checked all of its magazines well. When he was finished with that, he sharpened the bla of his combat knife. Most police officers did not carry figh ing knives, but almost everyone in his Tac Platoon did. Li combat infantrymen, they knew that when you really need a good knife, nothing in the world would substitute for Also a knife never needed to be reloaded.

Finally, Zumwald went over his six flash-bang grenade checking the pins and fuses to make sure that they we tightly screwed into the body. Then he taped the spoo down with black electrician's tape. That way, even if t pin snagged on something and pulled off, the spoon wouldr fly off. It was considered unhealthy to have a grenade spoc fly off when it was still in your ammo pouch.

When his weapons were ready, Zumwald turned to t rest of his personal gear.

His helmet radio had been gone over by the commo tech but he briefly turned it on and made a quick commo che with Dragon Control anyway just to test it. As always, was reading loud and clear.

He picked up his flak vest and pulled out each one of t ceramic inserts and checked to make sure that there we no cracks in them. A minute crack could make the diffe ence between the armored plates stopping a round or killi you. They too were all in order and he put them back his flak vest.

Lastly, he broke out his shoe shining gear and put a sp shine on the leather jump boots he would be wearing t morrow morning. He knew full well that they would g scuffed up as soon as he got in the back of the Griffin, b Zumwald was a Tac Cop and the platoon leader of the be damned Tactical Platoon in the entire force. He had a re utation to uphold and took pride in his appearance.

He still had to go over the Halo jump gear when it a rived, but it wasn't due in from the Army for several mor hours so he walked over to the officers' club for an earl dinner.

Even at this early hour, the small club was packed. Zum

wald wasn't the only chopper cop who had finished his mission preparations and found himself with time on his hands. He walked up to the bar and ordered a beer. He usually didn't drink before a mission, but one Lone Star wouldn't hurt anything.

Chapter 22

Bolen Air Base

The Dragon Flight air crew were waiting impatiently for the briefing when Wolff walked into the room with a thick folder under his arm. "Okay boys and girls," he said, striding up to the blackboard. "Here it is. We're going in at zero seven hundred tomorrow morning, locked and loaded."

"Excellent!" someone called out from the back row.

Wolff smiled. "Hold the applause," he said. "Until you've heard the details."

He clipped several large computer enhanced photographs up on the blackboard behind him. "This is it, the infamous Megaplatform."

He tapped a pointer on the photos of the oil collection facility. "And here is where we will hit first, the platform that controls the oil storage. The purpose of the exercise will be to deny them access to the oil so they can't pour any more of it into the Gulf."

He shifted the pointer to the next photo. "And then when that's been secured, we'll work on the central control platform next."

"Now, here's how we are going to do it. First off, One Zero and One Three will be the fire support ships for the mission."

He looked over at Gunner Jennings. "One Four and One

Two will be the troop lift ships. I'll have overall comman
and control for the mission and Gunner?"

"Yo!"

"You'll C and C the lift ships."

Jennings nodded.

"Okay, here's how it's going down. I'm taking a Hal
team in my ship up to ten thousand feet while the rest o
you sneak in under the radar."

"What the hell's a Halo Team?" Gunner frowned.

"High Altitude, Low Opening parachute team," Wol∎
grinned. "Zoomie and five of his maniacs are going to fre
fall and open their chutes five hundred feet above the o∎
containment platform."

"Jesus!"

"That's what I thought. Anyway . . ." Wolff continue∎
to lay out the plan in detail, assigning specific missions t∎
each of the Griffin crews.

"Now," he said when he was finished, "the key point of thi
operation is going to be flexibility. There's a dozen ways thi
thing can go bad on us, so you're going to have to stay rea∎
loose. Be prepared to shift your targets at a moment's notice."

"Any questions?"

There were a few points about coordination that neede∎
to be cleared up, but the chopper cops were true professionals. Even on a mission as complicated as this, they all kne∎
what they had to do. Wolff was just about to dismiss th∎
crews when Cuervo raised his hand. "What about me?" h∎
asked. 'Where do I go tomorrow?"

"Buzz says that he wants you in the TOC in case w∎
need to ask the Mexican authorities for assistance if any o∎
the bad guys get away from us." Wolff's voice was formal,
but there was no indication that he was dealing with Cuervo
in anything other than a professional manner.

Cuervo nodded. "Okay."

"Well," Wolff looked around the room. "If there's nothing else, I'm outa here."

* * *

Arturo Cuervo left the TOC after the air crew meeting and walked outside to the flight line with a sinking feeling in his gut. The sun was going down over the mesquite thickets and, even though a slight breeze had come up from the Gulf, it was still warm, but he shivered. It had all been for nothing. The role he had played, the risks he had taken, the stain to his honor as a policeman had all been for nothing.

From what he had heard in the briefing, it was obvious that the Tac Force was going to take back the Megaplatform regardless of the cost. No ransom was going to be paid and he would receive no payoff for the part he had played as Eagle, Cunningham's inside source of information.

When he had first been contacted by Cunningham, it had seemed to be a reasonable risk that would pay an extraordinary reward. Using his sources inside the Mexican Federal Police, he was to inform Cunningham about the security arrangements at certain American-owned Mexican oil rigs. Then, once he had become part of the plot, Cunningham had pressed him to develop sources inside the American Tac Force and Cuervo had had no choice but to comply.

Using his influence with high ranking officers in his own police force, it had been easy for him to be appointed as the liaison officer to the Tac Force during this emergency. And, once inside the Tac Force, it had been easy for him to get access to Dragon Flight's patrol schedule and pass it on to Cunningham. Here, the risk had been greater, but so had been the promised reward. Now, however, there would be no reward. There would be no payoff that would save his family's holdings for his younger brothers and sisters.

Arturo Cuervo was a man hard pressed by circumstances beyond his control. The drought in Central Mexico for the last two years had almost wiped out his family's extensive orchards and crops. They had been hit so hard that the land taxes were two years overdue and the Mexican government was in the process of foreclosing on the property for non-payment. Cuervo had been desperate and had seen Cunningham's scheme as a Heaven-sent way to get the money he needed to save his family's fortunes.

But it had not worked out that way. Once Cunningham had made the stupid mistake of ordering Falcon to attack his own refinery, the plan had gone bad. The oilman's occupation of the Megaplatform had only made a bad plan worse. Now that the Tac Force was ready to retake the oil rigs, Cuervo's dream of saving his family was dead and he had gambled his honor as a police officer for nothing.

He stood and looked out over the mesquite. He had even gambled away the friends he had made in the Tac Force. And, that bothered him more than he liked to admit. The men and women of Dragon Flight had welcomed him as a fellow professional police officer and had showed him true friendship.

He had betrayed their trust and now he did not even have the excuse of saving his family as a defense.

His mind racing, Cuervo turned and walked back to his room in the BOQ. There was still one last thing he had to do as Eagle. Something that might make amends for his betrayal of Dragon Flight.

Wolff walked into the club and sauntered over to where Gunner and Mugabe were standing at the bar. "Tequila," he ordered.

"I thought you'd quit doing that to yourself," Mugabe said.

"One more can't hurt me," Wolff grinned as he looked around the room. Sandra Revell was sitting at a table next to the window looking out over the flight line.

"Anyone seen Cuervo?' Wolff asked, casually.

"Nope," Mugabe answered. "Why?"

"Oh nothing," the pilot replied reaching for the shot of amber tequila. Holding a slice of lime in his other hand, he knocked the tequila back and bit into the lime.

"Good," he gasped.

Mugabe shuddered. "I hope you don't intend to keep that up tonight?"

Wolff laid his hand on his gunner's shoulder. "Gimme a break, Mojo. You know that I only have one drink on a night before a mission."

Mugabe looked up at his pilot. "Just checking," he said skeptically.

"Don't worry," Wolff said seriously. "I've never flown drunk or hungover in my life and I'm not about to start now." He laid the empty shot glass down on the bar. "Besides, I've got better things to do."

Mugabe followed Wolff's glance over to Legs' table. "Watch it now," he warned.

Wolff grinned and straightened the bottom of his leather flight jacket before walking across the dining room. "Mind if I join you?" he asked.

Sandra looked up in surprise. "Oh, Rick . . . Sure . . . sit down."

"You had dinner yet?" he asked.

She hesitated and glanced over to the door. "Not yet."

"I thought I'd find Cuervo here with you," Wolff said.

Sandra's eyes narrowed. "What do you mean by that?"

"Well," Wolff grinned boyishly. "The word is that you've become good friends." Wolff was unable to keep the sarcasm from his voice and she caught it.

"Look, Wolfman," her voice was even. "What I do on my off-duty time is my own business and I don't need anyone giving me a hard time about it. You got that?"

Wolff raised his hands in a gesture of peace. "Hold it," he said. "I just wanted to talk to him about something."

"I am expecting him," she admitted stiffly.

Wolff slid back his chair and stood up. "Well when you see him, can you tell him that I'd like a word with him about the mission."

She held her eyes steady on him for a moment. "Sure, I will."

"Thanks," he said turning to walk off.

"Oh Rick?"

"Yes."

She looked at him for a long moment. "Nothing," she said shaking her head.

Travis Cunningham III reached out to kill the modem hook up, the words "Eagle. Out" still glowed on the screen as it faded to black. The oilman smiled and leaned back in his chair, that wetback was really on the ball this time. For all of the public blustering about how tough the Tactical Police Force was, not even they were willing to risk more oil pollution in the Gulf of Mexico. He had them right by the balls and, by God, they knew it.

He got to his feet and headed down to find Falcon. For once the Arab had been wrong, the almighty Tac Force was just another bunch of federal pussies.

He found the Arab in the dayroom with De Lancy and the mercenary sergeant major, a South African named Bolls. The men were going over their defense plans one last time.

"Ya'll can put that away," Cunningham drawled. "I tole ya they wouldn't fuck with me."

"What do you mean?" Falcon asked.

"They're bringing the money tomorrow afternoon."

Falcon and De Lancy looked at one another. "Who told you that?" the Arab asked.

Cunningham smiled. "Eagle just called. That wetback has sure paid off for me." He laughed. "I'll have to see that he gets a little something extra in his paycheck."

"What happened to the Tac Force rule of never making ransom payments?"

Cunningham shrugged. "Beats the shit outa me. But like I said, them congressmen weren't about to do anything that would make me pour more oil into the Gulf. They've got an election year coming up and they don't want to do anything to make those folks along the Gulf coast mad at them.

"Anyway," Cunningham turned to go. "At three o'clock tomorrow afternoon, we're all going to be rich. They'll be callin' me at noon to set up the drop and the money's supposed to be here at three.

"So," Cunningham said as he opened the door. "Ya'll can just sit back and relax, Travis Cunningham has everything under control."

"What do you think?" De Lancy asked Falcon as soon as the oilman closed the door behind him.

The Arab thought for a moment. "I'm not sure. It does not sound like the same Tac Force I have heard about."

"But what if the local congressmen have brought political pressure to bear?"

"That may be, but I still do not trust them."

Falcon turned to the sergeant major. "Sergeant Major," he said. "Move the hostages to the hovercraft tonight."

"Sir."

"Keep it quiet, but have them moved before first light. Also, I want four of the missile gunners on the boat. Their orders are to save their missiles unless the boat is being directly attacked."

"Sir."

Falcon looked around the room, "Where's that rum of yours?" he asked De Lancy.

The mercenary reached into the side pocket of his pants and brought it out. "Do be careful, old man, that's all I have left."

"If this works, you will have all that you can possibly drink tomorrow night."

"Let's hope so," De Lancy said as he watched Falcon pour two fingers into a water glass. "It might get a bit sticky without it, what?"

Falcon took a slow sip. "It might get a bit 'sticky' anyway."

Chapter 23

Bolen Air Base

Dawn broke clear over the mesquite thickets along the Gulf Coast of Texas. The air was slightly chilly, a blue norther had come in during the night and had dropped the temperature, but the day promised to continue to be fair even if a bit colder than it had been the day before. It was a good day for an air assault. Even an air assault against a place as heavily defended as the Megaplatform.

As always, Mugabe greeted the dawn. Right as the sun came up, he was shocked to see his pilot come stumbling out of Red's maintenance office with a steaming cup of coffee held between his hands.

"Yo! Wolfman!" he shouted over to him. "What in the hell are you doing up at this early hour? You're supposed to still be in bed."

"Fuck you, Mojo," Wolff said as he slowly walked toward his partner. "Can't a man decide to change his ways if he wants to?"

"You can't," the black gunner laughed. "I know you too well."

"I couldn't sleep," Wolff explained, rubbing his hand across the back of his neck. "So I got up."

"Worried about the mission?"

"Shit, I don't know," Wolff shrugged. "This whole thing's been such a giant rat fuck right from the start that I don't know what I think anymore."

Mugabe was a little concerned to see the Wolfman talking that way. The main thing that gave Wolff his unbeatable edge in the air was his unshakable self-confidence. Sometimes he was overly confident, but it made him a fearless gunship driver. And flying a gunship into the face of enemy fire required that a man put his fears aside. To do otherwise could make a man turn away when the safest thing to do was to just keep on going and brave the fire.

"How about a little breakfast," Mugabe asked. "Some ham and eggs to get you going?"

"I'll pass," Wolff said, draining the last of his cup. "But I could use some more coffee."

"You do look like you're a quart low," Mugabe laughed.

"Fuck you, Mojo."

There were few people in the mess hall at this hour, but the cooks were standing by, ready to do their worst. "The crimes that are committed in the name of breakfast," Wolff muttered as he watched the cook break three egg yokes in a row trying to fry them over easy.

"If you can somehow manage to cook two of them without maiming them," the pilot said. "I'll take them and some hash browns that have actually been fried."

"Coming up," the cook said cheerfully.

Wolff got his breakfast, poured another cup of coffee and followed Mugabe to a table. "Did you see that guy?" Wolff muttered.

Mugabe stopped shoveling pancakes into his mouth. "Who?"

"The cook."

"What about him?"

"He was skinny, that's what," Wolff said, teasing the edge of an egg with his fork. "I never trust a skinny cook. If he doesn't eat his own cooking, why should I?"

"Good point," Mugabe agreed. "So, if you aren't going to eat those eggs, hand 'em over before they get cold."

Wolff slid his eggs onto Mojo's plate and watched him cut them up into his pancakes. "Jesus," he muttered softly, and went back to his coffee.

The other aircrews slowly filtered into the mess hall and braved the breakfast line. Some of them followed Mugabe's lead and ate heartily, but others could only face coffee before a mission, any mission. As they filed in, Wolff kept glancing up to see if Legs had arrived yet. Mugabe saw what he was doing, but didn't say anything. Of all mornings, this was not the time to get the Wolfman's mind locked onto anything but the upcoming mission.

"It's ten till," Mugabe said, glancing down at his watch. "We'd better get over to the TOC."

Wolff drained the last of his coffee, "Might as well do it," he said.

There wasn't much for Buzz to say at the six o'clock pilot's briefing. Everyone knew their assignments and he was confident that they would all do their jobs.

"Listen up," he said as he walked into the crowded room.

The room fell quiet as he walked up to the podium. "I'm not going to give you a pep talk," he said. "But there's a lot riding on this mission. We've got the Coast Guard and the Navy blockading the area and the Air Force is standing by with an AWAC in high orbit to help us control the operation and keep an eye out in case any more terrorists show up unannounced."

"Go Zoomies," someone in the back row muttered loud enough to be heard.

"We're in the spotlight again," Buzz continued as if he hadn't heard. "And we've got everyone from the head of the EPA to the senate minority leader watching to see how we pull this one off."

That got a few chuckles. Like it or not, maintaining an uncomfortably high profile was one of the things that the Tac Force did best. Every man knew that no matter what they did today, someone would find fault with it. If you were thin skinned or didn't like criticism, being a chopper cop was not the job for you.

"So to keep your glorious leader from having to testify in front of a senate investigation again, let's keep the damage to a minimum."

Someone laughed out loud. Buzz was famous for asking

senators embarrassing questions when they were on his case about one of Dragon Flight's operations.

"Are there any questions?" Buzz's eyes scanned the room.

There were none.

"Well then," he said. "Let's get out there and do it. Good luck and good hunting."

Lieutenant Arturo Cuervo peered around the side of the door to the pilots' locker room. The other air crews were gone, but Vargas and Johnson, the crew for One Three, were still changing into their flight gear. That was good, of all of the chopper cops, those were the two that he had not really made friends with. He instantly decided to put his backup plan into action.

The two men were at opposite ends of the room instead of standing close together. This was going to be a little more difficult than he had imagined, but if it worked, the payoff would be worth it. If he failed, however, he didn't even want to think about what would happen to him.

He quickly put the filter plugs in his nostrils and pulled a small aerosol canister from his pocket. Looking around to make sure that he was alone, he stepped out and walked up to the first man.

"Yo, Cuervo," Johnson turned when he saw him. "Aren't you going to stay . . ."

The aerosol knockout gas did its work in an instant and Johnson slumped to the floor. Vargas was halfway into his flight suit and looked up in surprise.

"Quick!" Cuervo said in alarm, as he bent down over the stricken man.

Vargas hitched up his uniform and ran over to his fallen co-pilot. Another blast of the gas put him on the floor beside Johnson.

Vargas was close to his size, so Cuervo quickly stripped the dark blue TPF flight suit from him and put it on over his tan Federale uniform. His flight helmet had been borrowed from Dragon Flight, so with the visor down, he could easily pass for Vargas. He also stripped Johnson's uniform and added his flight helmet to the pile before stuffing both men into their wall lockers and closing the doors behind them.

The extra uniform and helmet went into a flight bag along with all of the towels he could find lying around. Donning his flight helmet and snapping the visor down over his face, he left the locker room for the flight line.

Outside, Dragon One Three sat off to the side around the corner of the hangar. Red's people had had some last minute trouble with its commo gear and had pulled it over in front of the radio shop so the commo techs could have a go at it. Cuervo spotted it and had no trouble walking up to the helicopter unobserved. Opening the right side door, he climbed up into the pilot's seat and closed the door after him.

The flight suit and helmet he had stripped from Johnson was quickly stuffed with the towels from the locker room until it resembled a man. Strapped into the gunner's left seat, it should pass casual inspection and that was all he needed until he was in the air. Then, once the other Dragon Flight choppers were engaged at the Megaplatform, he would be able to make his escape in the chopper.

Vargas, the pilot of One Three, had been raised in the northeastern United States along the Canadian border and had what could be mistaken for a British accent. Although Cuervo spoke good American English, he had been educated in British schools and could affect the accent whenever he wanted. He was certain that he could pass for the pilot on the radio. The fact that the replacement pilots had not been flying with Dragon Flight very long should help with the deception.

As he started the pre-flight checklist, he tried not to think about the fact that he was stealing a helicopter from people who had made him feel so welcome. But it was quite obvious that he was not going to get a payoff from Cunningham, the Tac Force was going to make sure that the oilman did not receive his ransom. Cuervo had to raise money for his family somehow and a TPF Griffin should bring quite a sum on the weapons black market. Probably about twice as much as the oilman had promised him for acting as Eagle.

He hoped that his last transmission as Eagle would help make amends for his treachery. If Cunningham thought that the Tac Force was scheduled to pay the ransom by mid-afternoon, he would not be expecting them to attack, particularly not in the morning. He knew that it wasn't much to atone for what he had done, but it might help Dragon Flight catch Cunningham's mercenaries unaware and make their job a little easier. Particularly since they would have to do it with one less gunship to support their attack.

He forced these thoughts out of his mind as he quickly completed the Griffin's pre-flight checklist. Wolff had done a good job of checking him out on the gunship and he flew through the procedure without a hitch.

"Dragon Flight, this is Dragon Lead," came Wolff's voice in his head phones. "Show time, crank 'em."

"One Three, copy," Cuervo radioed back as he twisted the throttle open to flight idle and pulled the starting trigger on the collective control stick. The starboard turbine whined as the starter motor spun it over and then ignited with a soft roar. Keeping his eyes on the instruments, Cuervo switched over to the other turbine and it fired up as well. As soon as both turbines spooled up and brought the main rotor up to speed, he clicked in the throat mike. "One Three, go."

"Dragon Control," he heard Wolff radio. "This is Lead. We're ready to roll."

"This is Control," Mom answered. "You are cleared for take off."

"Lead, copy," Wolff answered as he brought his ship up in a low ground effect hover and pointed its nose for the runway. "Dragon Flight, this is Lead, roll 'em."

Cuervo waited his turn before taxiing out onto the runway, As he passed by the hangar, he saw the Tac Force

151

ground crew watching their ships go off to battle. They're a good bunch, he thought briefly, I'm going to miss them.

The four Griffins paused briefly at the end of the runway to get their interval before starting their take off runs. Less than ten meters apart, the four loaded down gunships started down the runway, their tails high and the fronts of their skids inches off the ground in a classic gunship takeoff. As their speed came up, Wolff broke in on the chopper-to-chopper radio net. "Dragon Flight, this is Lead," he radioed. "On my command, pull pitch now!"

As if tied together with ropes, the four Griffins of Dragon Flight rose up into the air as if they were one machine. Forming up in a line formation over the airfield, Wolff led the sleek ships on one fly-by over the hangar before turning south and setting course for the Gulf of Mexico and their appointment with the Megaplatform.

At the tail end Charlie position at the rear of the formation, Cuervo sat back and was able to relax for the first time this morning.

It had worked. He had gotten off the ground safely and now that he was in the air, he was almost home free.

Chapter 24

The Megaplatform

On the Megaplatform, Cunningham was running around in an uncontrolled frenzy, trying to supervise everything all at once. Believing that the Tac Force was finally going to pay him off had caused the oilman to become even more irrational than he had been before. His excitement was at a fever pitch, but Falcon finally convinced him to go up into the control room and leave the preparations to him. But even with Cunningham's unbridled enthusiasm, Falcon went to find De Lancy.

The mercenary captain was in the pilothouse of the hovercraft that had been moored alongside the central control platform under the deck overhang. "How's the fat Yank this morning?" De Lancy greeted him.

The Arab shook his head. "He is acting like a boy who is hopping from one foot to the other while he waits to visit his first whorehouse."

De Lancy laughed.

"But I do not share his optimism," Falcon frowned. "I may be wrong, but I do not think that the Tac Force is going to give in to him that easily."

"Do you think that Eagle's last message was a subterfuge?"

Falcon stared out over the water. "I don't know. It is possible that Eagle was compromised and the Tac Force sent the message themselves. But whatever, I am not going to sit by and wait to see what really happens this afternoon before I do something. In fact, I want you to send one of our helicopters up as soon as possible to give us early warning of their approach."

De Lancy reached for the radio phone and quickly gave the order.

"How are our hostages doing?" Falcon asked.

"Just fine," De Lancy said with a grin. "I don't think that Cunningham even knows that I transferred them over here last night."

"Good," Falcon said. "I have a feeling that we are going to need them today. I want this boat ready to move at a moment's notice. I want to be underway as soon as I see the first Tac Force gunship start shooting."

"I'll have the sergeant major tell my cadre to stay close."

"Do that," the Arab said. "Because if this goes the way I think it will, there will be no time for us to wait for them. The only way that you and I will keep from ending up in a cell alongside Cunningham is if we move fast."

De Lancy shuddered. Prison was not high on his list of

favorite places. "Don't worry," he said. "If it goes wrong, I'll be the first one on the boat."

"The second one," Falcon said dryly.

De Lancy laughed.

"Dragon Lead," came Mom's voice over the command net radio. "This is Dragon Control. Send status, we haven't heard from you and we are uptight here. How copy?"

In the left hand seat, Mugabe's head snapped around to look at Wolff. The use of the word 'Uptight' in a normal transmission was an emergency code to switch to the scrambled communications mode. It meant that their normal tactical communications network had been compromised and someone was listening in to their radio traffic.

Wolff quickly switched over to scramcomm. "Dragon Lead on scramcomm one. go."

"This is Control, be advised that an unauthorized pilot is flying Dragon One Three. How copy?"

Wolff was stunned. "This is Lead, say again."

"This is Control," Mom sounded calm. "I say again. Vargas and Johnson were just discovered unconscious in their wall lockers at the base. Dragon One Three is being flown by an intruder. How copy?"

'Intruder' was the code word for an unauthorized person loose in a TPF facility. Intruders were always considered to be armed and dangerous.

"Lead, good copy," Wolff paused as something clicked into place in his mind. "Has anyone seen Lieutenant Cuervo lately?"

"Control, wait one."

"Lead this is Command One," Buzz's voice broke in a moment later. "Be advised that no one has seen Cuervo since you took off. How copy?"

"This is Lead, good copy," Wolff radioed back. "What are your instructions?"

"This is Command One," Buzz's voice was hard. "Regardless of who's flying One Three, it is imperative that you continue the mission. Washington is very concerned. How copy?''

"Lead, good copy."

"Command One, negative further."

"Lead, clear."

"Now what the fuck do we do?" Mugabe asked.

Wolff looked out the windscreen for a moment. So this was what it had been all about. This was why Cuervo had worked so hard to get in the good graces of the men and women of Dragon Flight. He was a fucking hijacker.

He slowly shook his head. "I'll be double fucked if I know, Mojo."

Wolff had lucked out in one regard, Dragon One Three was one of the two fire support choppers for this mission and wasn't carrying troops. But of course, Cuervo would have been careful not to try to hijack a chopper with an armed TPF Tac Team in the back. That meant that if Wolff could somehow alert the crews of the other two choppers, they could still try to carry out the mission while they kept an eye on the renegade gunship.

The real question was what Cuervo intended to do with his stolen machine. If he only intended to try to escape with it, they could deal with that. But if he tried to disrupt the attack on the terrorists, that was an entirely different matter.

Wolff keyed his throat mike. "One Four, this is Lead."

"One Four, go," came Gunner's voice in his headphones.

"This is Lead," Wolff said casually. "Watch your interval, we're getting uptight over here. How Copy?"

"This is One Four. Good copy."

A second later, Gunner's voice came in over the scramcomm. "What the fuck's going on, Wolfman?"

"We've got us a little problem here," Wolff explained. "I just got a call from Buzz. They discovered Vargas and Johnson stuffed into their wall lockers back at the base."

"Who the hell's flying One Three?"

"Cuervo."

"Shit!" Gunner said softly. "What are you going to do now?"

"Buzz said that we have to continue the mission as best we can." Wolff radioed back. "But we've got to keep a close eye on that bastard at the same time until we find out what he's planning to do with our chopper."

"That's going to leave us real short on fire power," Gunner said grimly.

"I know," Wolff replied. "But that's the way Buzz wants it. The mission comes first."

"Okay," Gunner said. "But the first time that guy makes a wrong move, I'm going to blow his ass out of the sky."

"Only if you get to him before I do," Wolff said. "When he makes his move, go to clear channel and let me know what he's doing."

"You got it," Gunner replied.

In the left seat of Dragon One Four, Sandra Revell was shocked as she listened in on Wolff and Gunner's scrambled conversation. Arturo had stolen a Griffin? It didn't seem possible, but she knew that Buzz would not have called unless it was a fact. She turned around in her seat and tried to spot One Three at the end of the formation, but she couldn't see him.

When Gunner ended his call to Wolff, he turned and looked over at her. "We're probably going to have to kill that guy," he stated flatly. The big question of whether she would be able to fire on him or not was left unstated, but she knew that it was there.

She reached forward, flicked on her turret weapon controls and turned back to face her pilot. "You put me in a firing position," she said without emotion. "And I'll splash the intruder."

Jennings nodded and went back to flying the ship. He expected no less from whoever was flying in his left seat.

Sandra sat and stared out the windscreen at Wolff's One Zero in front of them. Suddenly, her life had become more complicated. She had been right the first time, it didn't pay to mix her personal life with her work. And, in this case, even a visiting Mexican police officer who she had never expected to see again had become work. She tightened the fingers of her nomex gloves, ready to get the job done.

When they were still an hour away from the Megaplatform, Dragon Flight headed for the deck and Wolff broke away from them and climbed up to ten thousand feet. The other Griffins would make their approach on the wave tops while Wolff changed his heading so he could rendezvous with the Navy patrol plane that had been keeping an eye on the oil rig. As he flew, he switched on the radar transponder that had been pre-set to the Navy patrol plane's frequency.

Whoever Cunningham had in the Megaplatform control tower would pick him up on the approach radar. But hopefully, with the transponder squawking on the Navy frequency, they would think that his chopper was merely a replacement for the airborne surveillance plane. The limited radar equipment in the control tower would fix on the transponder, so it wouldn't matter if the Griffin's radar signature was not exactly the same as the Navy planes they had been tracking.

In the back of Dragon One Zero, Zumwald and his men checked over their Halo jump gear one last time. Since they were jumping from 10,000 feet they didn't need oxygen equipment, but they were still laden with their weapons, ammunition and the jump gear itself.

The one thing that Zumwald checked twice was the altimeter he would use to determine the distance above the platform when he and his team would open their chutes. He planned to open them at the last possible moment to decrease the amount of time that they would be hanging helplessly in the sky, so it had to be right on. Just a few feet off and they would either slam into the platform, their chutes not yet fully deployed, or be sitting ducks hanging under their canopies.

"Wolfman," he called up on the intercom. "What's your altitude reading?"

"We're holding steady at ten thousand, ninety-seven feet above sea level."

"Thanks." Zumwald set the numbers and locked his altimeter. He also set the numbers in the tiny altitude radar unit on his jump harness. It would give him an absolute height readout over his target in case anything went wrong with the altimeter.

When everything had been double checked, the Tac Platoon leader tried to relax, but it was not easy. He had made parachute jumps into hot spots before, but this was a first for him, a Halo drop onto a defended position. In fact, it was probably a first in police annals. Army Rangers and Special Forces units used Halo equipment, but the idea of police officers dropping down on the bad guys from ten thousand feet was completely new.

He smiled to himself when he thought of his name going down in the books as the man who had led the first Halo jump in police history. Even if the operation went tits up and they got blasted from the sky on the way down, he would still go down in the books.

He sat back against the rear bulkhead of the chopper and tried to relax. One way or the other, he was going to make history today.

Chapter 25

High Over the Gulf

"We're five minutes from the drop zone, Zoomie," Wolff called back on the intercom.

"Copy, we're getting ready now." Zumwald slid back the side doors and signaled for his team to put on their protective masks and take up their jump positions in the open doors.

Zumwald and the five jumpers split up, three men on each side, and sat down on the floor plates with their feet on the chopper's skids. The blast from the main rotor buffeted their helmeted heads, but they would be out of the blast in a few seconds, free falling through the clear Texas sky at a hundred and twenty miles an hour.

"Sixty seconds," Wolff called back. "Fifty, forty . . ."

When the count reached zero, Zumwald shouted "Airborne" and flung himself into the empty air away from the chopper. He instantly assumed a spread eagle, skydiving position and looked back to see that the rest of his team had exited the helicopter and were stacked up above him.

Unlike civilian skydivers, the Tac Team did not link up and fall together. Instead they assumed positions one above the other like a stick of human bombs falling to earth. Zumwald tucked his arms and legs in tighter, increasing his diving speed as much as he dared, and the others followed suit at over a hundred and twenty miles an hour. In a few seconds, they would be in position to deploy their chutes.

As soon as the jumpers were clear, Wolff shoved forward on the cyclic control stick and sent the Griffin into a dive. In the left seat, Mugabe activated his targeting radar and flipped the switch to arm the nose turret weapons. He dialed the ammunition selection feed to a mix of AP tracer and HE for the 25mm and flash-bang grenades mixed with tear gas for the 40mm.

"Bear one six three," he called the target data over to the pilot.

"I've got visual contact," Wolff answered watching the small shape of the terrorists' Super Puma growing larger by the second.

The hard part wasn't going to be aceing the Puma, that would be a piece of cake. The mercenary pilots had no idea that the Griffin was coming down on top of them. And even if they were picked up on the air traffic control radar and a warning was sent, Wolff still had the altitude on them. In aerial combat, altitude equals advantage.

The hard part of this exercise was going to be getting down to the platform in time to clear an area for the jumpers to land after they destroyed the Puma. Wolff was diving on the Puma at well over two hundred and fifty miles an hour, but Zumwald's free falling Tac Team was right behind them moving at a hundred and twenty. He only had time for one quick pass at the Puma before he had to start his strafing run over the platform to clear it for the Tac Team's landing.

Mugabe started firing at the terrorists' chopper from four thousand meters out, the maximum range for the Chain Gun. Using the visual sight as well as the radar lock-on, Mugabe's first rounds were right on target. Ten times a second the Chain Gun's stabilizer automatically re-aimed the gun, insuring that Mugabe stayed on target.

Far below them, the dark green Super Puma staggered under the pounding of the 25mm. Wolff saw the sparkle of the HE rounds exploding on the Puma's turbine housing and the pieces of metal torn off by the explosions and blown back into the slip stream.

A second burst found the fuel tanks as the Puma nosed over and headed for the Gulf of Mexico. Her main rotor still spinning, the Super Puma trailed fire as she crashed into the water. Wolff snapped One Zero out of its dive and banked over to line up with the oil collection platform.

Falcon's mercenaries were alert, the instant after the Puma blossomed in flame, Mugabe's threat radar picked up a missile launch.

"Launch! Launch!" he shouted, his fingers stabbing at the decoy flare launch button on the counter-measures panel.

Out in the open the way they were, they were sitting ducks. The only thing that would save them was if Mugabe could get the heat seeking guidance system on the missile to lock-on to a decoy flare. The flare burned at ten thousand degrees, a hundred times as hot as the turbine exhausts of the Griffin. When the missile's guidance system saw the hotter flares, it would track them instead of following the helicopter. As soon as the flares were away, the gunner triggered off another pair, one to each side of the Griffin.

Wolff caught a glimpse of the missile's smoke trail to his right and he slammed the gunship over onto its left side, putting the chopper's belly to the missile and hiding the turbine exhausts from the heat seeking warhead. Even with the Black Hole heat suppressor kits mounted on the turbines, there was still danger.

The violent maneuver unloaded the rotor head, causing the blades to lose lift and the Griffin dropped like a stone.

Wolff dumped his collective to bring the rotor RPM back up and dropped his nose right as the missile flashed past them in a clean miss. Its IR heat seeking warhead locked onto one of the decoy flares. This missile, however, also had a small radar unit in the war head that controlled a proximity detonator. And, as it passed by the Griffin, the radar kicked in and it exploded anyway.

The detonation of the missile warhead shook the diving chopper and Wolff heard pings as fragments hit the airframe. But the pilot paid it no mind and banked his ship over to line up for his firing run over the oil collection platform. Zumwald's team would be popping their chutes any second now and he could see camouflaged figures running for their defensive positions as he bore down on them. He had to get the landing zone cleared for Zoomie's Tac Team.

"Get 'em, Mojo!" he shouted.

Mugabe's fingers tightened around his firing controls as he triggered the 40mm grenade launcher in the nose turret. A stuttering cough sounded as the 40mm sprayed tear gas and flash-bang grenades at a rate of three hundred rounds a minute. Mugabe swung the turret from side to side, blanketing the entire platform and then turned it all the way around so he could continue firing as Wolff threw the Griffin into a hard banking turn high over the platform.

No sooner had the first tear gas rounds blossomed on the deck of the platform, than Zumwald's men suddenly appeared five hundred feet above it. Their white chutes blossomed in the clear blue sky like six square clouds hanging over the Gulf of Mexico.

Pulling on their risers, the Tac Team guided their steerable chutes in to a landing on the helipad in the middle of the platform. A foot off the deck, Zumwald punched the chute release in the center of his harness and rolled into a parachute landing fall. He came out of the roll with his MP-5 in his hands spitting 9mm rounds.

Even with the tear gas blanketing the platform, the mercenaries fought back fiercely. Automatic weapons fire swept the helipad landing zone and one of the Tac Team took a bullet when he hit the deck, his grunt of pain sounding in Zumwald's earphones.

The platoon leader was too busy returning fire to look around to see who had been hit. Their only hope now was to overwhelm the defenders.

He dropped an empty magazine and slammed a fresh one in its place as he dashed for cover behind a pile of oil pipes at the side of the helipad. A mercenary, his eyes streaming tears, popped up from behind the pipes right in front of him. Zumwald gunned him down before the man even had a chance to bring his weapon to bear.

One for us, Zoomie thought.

* * *

High in the control room in the tower on the central platform, Cunningham screamed in rage when Wolff's Griffin dropped out of the sky and made its strafing run over the oil collection facility. "God damn you!" He pounded his fists on the control panel.

He ran for the other end of the master control panel and hit the switch for the oil pumps on the containment tanks. "Bastards!"

When the red light came on indicating that the pumps were in operation, he ran back to the window to watch the black oil pour into the Gulf. "I told you bastards not to fuck with me!" he screamed.

Zumwald was pinned down behind the stack of steel pipes when he heard the throbbing whine as the oil pumps came on. He was still twenty feet from the emergency shutoff controls. Twenty feet of open ground covered with automatic weapons fire from the mercenaries' positions. He was so close, but yet so far away.

He dropped the partial magazine from his MP and clipped a full one into the magazine well and took a deep breath. This was where he was really going to earn his hazardous duty pay. The ten thousand foot Halo drop had been nothing compared to this. This shit was serious!

He keyed his helmet mike, "Tac One this is Zoomie!" he radioed to his team. "Cover me, I'm going for the control panel!"

He gathered his feet under him and waited until the volume of fire from his team reached an ear-shattering crescendo. Firing short bursts from the hip, he jumped up and dashed out into the open, sprinting for the control panel. Bullets sang past him as he ran and he answered them with short bursts of his own.

Six feet from safety, he felt a blow to the chest and a sharp pain in his right side. Another blow took his right leg out from under him and he crashed to the steel deck, his

MP-5 flying from his suddenly nerveless fingers and skidding out of reach. Fumbling at his holster with his left hand, he drew the 10mm Glock pistol and flicked it off safety.

Rolling over, he triggered three quick shots at the mercenaries on the other side of the helipad. The boom of the big 10mm sounded clear over the rattle of the smaller caliber weapons. He continued rolling and firing until he was safely behind the steel cabinet of the control panel. He didn't even bother to stop and catch his breath. He painfully pulled himself up until he could reach the emergency pump shut down controls. Grabbing the red handle with his good hand, he hauled down on it, cutting the electrical power to the pumps.

The throbbing sound of oil being pumped into the Gulf stopped abruptly.

He keyed his helmet mike. "Dragon Lead," he radioed up to Wolff. "This is Tac One, I'm hit, but I've got the pumps turned off and I'm under cover."

"Copy," Wolff radioed back. "Hang on Zoomie, we're coming down to get you."

When Falcon saw the burning Puma plummet down from the sky, he realized that the Tac Force gunships had arrived. And, as he had feared, they had arrived with their guns blazing. His employer had just run out of options and it was high time for the mercenary to look to his own safety. As he ran for the hovercraft's pilothouse, he pulled the radio from his belt and keyed the mike, "De Lancy!" he shouted. "Now!"

Without waiting for the De Lancy and the men who were going with him, Falcon started up the powerful engines of the hovercraft and prepared to make his desperate run for freedom. For the next few minutes, the Tac Force would be occupied trying to get a foothold on the platforms and hopefully he could get away in the confusion.

De Lancy raced up to the wheel house, a shoulder fired

missile in his hands. "Go!" he shouted and raced back down onto the deck.

Falcon saw that the lines were cast off and, with a quick prayer to Allah, advanced his throttles.

The hovercraft rose on the power of her fans until the skirts were just brushing the wave tops as the Arab turned the bow away from the platform. By ducking in and out of the cover of the other platforms, he would try to make his way to the outer edge of the complex before making his break for the open water.

Chapter 26

The Megaplatform

When Wolff racked his ship around to go back to help Zumwald, the other three attacking choppers of Dragon Flight swept in right above the wave tops heading straight for the platforms. Splashing the mercenaries' Puma had destroyed the element of surprise and it was time to get down to serious work.

Gunner Jennings' Dragon One Four, followed One Two as the two gunships broke away and headed for their first objective, the central control platform. Zooming up to the level of the deck, One Two sprayed tear gas and flash-bang grenades at the mercenary positions along the catwalks surrounding the platform. Camouflaged figures scattered for cover under the gunship's attack.

Coming in low, Gunner hauled up on his collective at the last possible moment to pull pitch. One Four leaped up in the air like a rabbit to the level of the helipad on the main deck. Pulling the chopper's nose up sharply to flare out and kill his forward momentum, the pilot skidded his Griffin to a stop at the edge of a circle of oil drums blocking the center of the landing site.

"Go! Go! Go!' he shouted to the men in the back.

Sandra kept up a steady covering fire of flash-bang grenades and 25mm while the Tac Team jumped down to the deck and scrambled for cover behind the obstacles. As soon as the last man was clear of his ship, Gunner hauled up sharply on his collective. The lightened Griffin leaped skyward, away from the streams of terrorist return fire flashing across the open deck.

Sandra tried to cover their escape with her guns, but there was a split second before Gunner could shove his nose down and make his escape. And in that brief instant, a burst of fire hit the Griffin's armored cockpit. A second burst tore into the portside turbine nacelle.

Gunner frantically tried to evade the fire and still give Sandra an opening to use her guns as well, but it wasn't working. He didn't have any airspeed built up yet and the mercenaries had their range. Their bullets flashed as they ricocheted off the Griffin's armor plating. But even with the armor protecting them, Gunner heard a couple of rounds hit home in the chopper's unprotected airframe.

From his position well back from the attacking gunships, Cuervo saw Gunner's Dragon One Four take fire. He also saw that Gunner's wingman and fire support ship, One Two, was too far out of position to come to his aid in time.

The Mexican quickly switched on the pilot's override to the weapons controls so he could fire the turret weapons from the right seat. Twisting the throttle up against the stop, he pulled pitch to bring his ship up into position to go to Gunner and Sandra's aid.

He had not forgotten about making his escape. He was a rogue now, but he was still enough of a police officer to go to the assistance of another officer in trouble. Every cop responds to another officer under fire, regardless of the circumstances.

Locking the nose turret in the straight ahead position, he activated his HUD sight in his helmet visor, aimed at the catwalk on the near side of the platform and pulled the Chain Gun's trigger on the cyclic control stick. The Griffin's airframe shook as the 25mm in the nose turret spit heavy caliber fire.

Nudging down on the rudder pedal, Cuervo walked his line of fire across the catwalk. The explosive fire sent the mercenaries scrambling for cover and ended the deadly streams of fire from their positions aimed at Gunner and Sandra. Out of the corner of his eye, he saw Gunner back away and run for safety, but Cuervo still kept boring in, his nose turret flashing flame.

He was only a few hundred meters out from the edge of the platform when he saw a lone figure step out on the walkway around the rooftop of the control tower. The man was wearing civilian clothes and carried a shoulder fired rocket launcher in his hands. The pilot instinctively stomped down on the right rudder pedal and slammed the cyclic control stick all the way over against the right stop.

The Griffin heeled over onto her right side as Cuervo brought the nose turret to bear. Triggering off a quick burst of 25mm as he flashed by, he saw the figure take a hit right as he swung the launcher up to his shoulder. Most of his poorly aimed burst missed, but one powerful 25mm round smashed through the launcher and exploded, flinging the man's body off the back side of the tower like a rag doll.

Cuervo did not even recognize that it was his late employer whom he had just blown away.

When the Mexican pilot saw that Gunner and Sandra were completely in the clear, he dropped the nose of his Griffin and banked away.

As Wolff racked his gunship around to make another pass in support of Zoomie's men on the oil control platform, he caught a glimpse of Cuervo's gun run on the central platform. The big white number 13 painted on the Griffin's dark blue nose left no doubt in his mind as to who was behind the controls of the ship. He didn't know what in the hell was going on, but he had no time to worry about it now. At least, Gunner had someone backing up his play.

Wolff snapped the tail of his ship around and Mugabe opened up again, walking his fire into the few remaining mercenaries on the oil control platform. So far, the defenders were reeling from the sudden onslaught of the Griffin and were only offering scattered return fire.

With the Mugabe's covering fire supporting them, Zoomie's men charged across the open deck and took up positions close enough to use their stun grenades. Several of the small black canisters tumbled through the air to explode with a blinding flash and an ear-shattering blast.

Before the smoke had time to clear, the black clad Tac Team got to their feet and charged.

Up on the deck of the speeding hovercraft, De Lancy and his missile gunners held their fire as Falcon maneuvered the craft in between the oil rigs on his way to the open sea. They would only fire their Bee Sting missiles if the gunships threatened them. But so far, the TPF Griffins were completely occupied with their assault on the platforms. None of them had seemed to notice them making their escape and that was the way Falcon wanted it. In a few more seconds, they would be in the clear.

The craft's hover fans were set at full pitch and the turbines were screaming at full throttle as they raced across the wave tops at over eighty knots, ducked in between the legs of the last platform. Right on the other side, lay the open waters of the Gulf and their hoped-for sanctuary in the Cayman Islands.

Down on the oil collection platform, Wolff watched as the camouflaged figures of the mercenaries came out of their positions with their hands held high in the air and slowly walked out into the open. The black uniformed Tac Team quickly disarmed them, cuffed their hands behind their backs and sat them down in an easily guarded group in the middle of the helipad.

"Dragon Lead, this is Tac One," Zumwald radioed up to the pilot a moment later. "I've got the platform under control now. I also have five wounded down here, two friendlies and three suspects. Two of them are priority and we need medevac ASAP. How copy?"

"This is Dragon Lead. Good copy. Be advised that Dustoff medevac is on station. I'll send it your way ASAP."

"Tac One, good copy."

Wolff switched channels on the ship's radios. "Dragon Control, this is Lead. We need Dustoff ASAP on the oil collection platform. How Copy?"

"This is control, good copy," Mom responded. "We monitored Tac One's message. Dustoff is on the way. Be prepared to pop smoke on call."

"This is Lead," Wolff said. "Have him contact Tac One for final approach."

"Control, good copy. Clear."

Just then, Mugabe caught a glimpse of the hovercraft breaking cover at the outer ring of the platforms. "Wolfman!" he shouted. "Eleven o'clock!"

The pilot snapped his head around in time to see the hovercraft head out into open water at high speed. He also saw the camouflaged figures of De Lancy and his men on the upper deck. Twisting his throttle up against the stop, he banked his Griffin over and dropped the nose to gain speed.

"Dragon Flight!" he shouted over the radio. "This is Lead! There's a hovercraft to the south trying to make a run for it. Stop them!"

"One Two, copy. I'm right behind you."

"One Four," Gunner radioed. "I took some fire, I'll be there in a second."

Now that he was in the clear, Gunner wanted to check over his aircraft to see if he had sustained any damage from

169

the ground fire before he went into battle again. Both turbines were in the green, the oil pressure was okay and the exhaust gas temperature gauges also showed green. Beyond a few cracks in the bulletproof Lexan plastic of the canopy, the Griffin seemed to be okay.

Now he could look around and see how the battle was going.

Cuervo had been monitoring the Dragon Flight radio net and now that everyone else was engaged, he saw this as his opportunity to make his move. He reached down to flick the RPM governor switch over to increase and the turbines screamed at a hundred and ten percent power. He brought the Griffin down low over the waves again and banked away to the west, away from the hovercraft.

With the screaming turbines on over-rev, he would be out of the battle area in seconds. And once he got a minute or two head start, the other Griffins would never be able to catch up with him.

In the pilothouse of the speeding hovercraft, Falcon saw the dark shapes of the sleek Griffins wheel away from the distant oil rigs and drop down as they headed straight for his boat.

"De Lancy!" he shouted through the open window. "Look out!"

The mercenary captain spun around, spotted the gunships and shouted orders to his missile gunners. The four mercenaries hoisted the Bee Sting missile launchers up to their shoulders and activated their heat seeking target tracking systems.

"As soon as you can get a lock on them," De Lancy yelled over the roar of the hover fans. "Fire!"

* * *

Gunner easily spotted the speeding hovercraft with the two Griffins in hot pursuit and was banking over to join them when he spotted the small dark shape of Cuervo's Griffin low against the water. The renegade was heading away from the fight as fast as the machine would fly.

"Lead," Gunner radioed. "This is One Four. The intruder is making a run for it!"

"This is Lead," Wolff quickly radioed back. "Don't let him get away!"

"One Four, copy."

Chapter 27

The Gulf of Mexico

A grim-faced Wolff unconsciously twisted the throttle even harder up against the stop, trying to get even more speed out of the howling turbines. Now that Cuervo had finally made his move and Gunner was chasing after him, he only had Dragon One Two to help him bring the hovercraft down. And if the mercenaries decided to turn and fight and defended themselves with their missiles, someone was sure as hell going to get hurt in the process.

"We've got heat seeking missiles tracking us!" Mugabe suddenly shouted, his finger reaching for the decoy flare launcher button on the counter measures panel.

Wolff ignored the warning and bored on in closer. He couldn't let the hovercraft get away. He switched the radio over to the international emergency frequency and keyed his helmet microphone. "This is the United States Tactical Police Force," he transmitted. "Stop your hovercraft now and return to the . . ."

"Launch!" Launch!" Mugabe shouted, his finger stabbing down on the flare launcher button.

Gunner slammed his ship over into a sharply banked turn to take up pursuit of the renegade gunship. Cuervo had a couple of minutes head start on him and it would be difficult to catch up with him now. But the Mexican pilot hadn't had the endless hours behind the controls of a Griffin that Gunner had put in. Even though the two ships were identical and theoretically had the same top speed, there were a few tricks about flying a Griffin that Cuervo simply had not had the time to learn yet. This was one of those times when the details counted and would determine the outcome of the race.

The first thing he had to do was to drop all of his underwing ordnance. The added weight and drag would hold him back too much and all he really needed for an air to air dog fight was the nose turret weapons. "Drop the ordnance," he ordered.

Sandra reached out and toggled the under wing hard point release switches. The rocket pods and their pylons fell away and she could feel the ship immediately gain speed.

As soon as the rocket pods were gone, Gunner reached down to the side control console, flicked the RPM governor control to increase and twisted the throttle up against the stop. The twin GE turbines screamed like banshees.

Feathering the collective pitch control, he set the main rotor blades as fine as they could go and still provide enough additional lift to keep the ship in the air. At this speed, the screaming turbine exhausts were providing most of the ship's forward thrust and the stubwings were creating most of her lift.

He nudged forward on the cyclic stick and brought the gunship down until the skids were skimming a bare inch or two above the wave tops. A rotary winged aircraft flies best in dense air and it just didn't get any denser than down at absolute wave top level.

The gunship was flying a good twenty-five miles an hour

faster than the designers had ever intended her to fly. And if Gunner kept the RPM governor on increase for too long, the turbines would trash themselves. Red would shit a brick, but Gunner really didn't care, he'd deal with the maintenance chief when the time came. Right now, he was slowly gaining on Cuervo's stolen ship and that was all that counted. He could not let him get away with that Griffin.

In the left seat, Sandra dialed in AP and HE ammunition for the Chain Gun as she watched the red range numbers slowly change in her radar weapons sight. Suddenly, the radar readout went crazy. The range numbers flashed off and on, and the sight picture of the fleeing Griffin disintegrated into a jumbled blur.

"Fuck!" she yelled over to Gunner. "He's switched on his ECM!"

Part of the military equipment built into the Griffin's gunnery systems was an Electronic Counter Measures module designed to prevent an enemy getting a radar lock on. By broadcasting a jamming signal on the same frequency that the targeting radar used, the ECM module scrambled the return signal and rendered it useless.

"Goddamn that Wolff for showing him all of our stuff," Gunner muttered grimly. "He sure as hell knows that we're on to him now."

Sandra switched her targeting radar off and activated her optical weapons sight. She was not as good a bare eyeball shooter as Mugabe was, but she had proven on the firing range that she could still hold her own when the radar units were down. Sandra tightened her fingers back around the firing controls.

Gunner was slowly gaining on the speeding Dragon One Three. In another minute or two they would be within range to open fire on him. Sandra still wasn't sure what she was going to do when she had the renegade Mexican in her sights, but she knew that they couldn't let Cuervo get away.

Not while he was stealing a Griffin.

If the sophisticated police gunship got into the wrong hands, it could cause the deaths of countless innocent people

173

and she didn't want to have something like that on her conscience.

At Mugabe's warning of a missile launch, Wolff rolled the Griffin over onto her side and banked away to turn his belly to the heat seeking missile and hide the heat from his turbine exhausts. Even though the Black Hole IR emissions shields were fitted to the exhausts and Mugabe was firing decoy flares, he wasn't going to sit there and wait to see if they were enough to save them.

Right behind Wolff, Dragon One Two executed the same maneuver as the twin streaks of dirty white smoke followed the missiles into the air. Both of them, however, locked onto the hotter IR tracks of the decoy flares and didn't even come close enough for the proximity fuses to detonate.

Wolff had no time to congratulate himself, however, the second two missiles were launched an instant later and streaked up at them. Again, Mugabe fired more decoy flares, but this time, one of the missiles exploded close enough to them to rock the ship and send warhead fragments smashing into the air frame.

When Wolff saw that the mercenaries had dropped their empty missile launchers and were bringing up their assault rifles, he bore back down onto them. "Missed, you assholes," the pilot growled as he dropped down into a gun run. "Now it's my turn."

With Wolff throwing the Griffin around in the sky to dodge the storm of automatic weapons fire rising from the boat, Mugabe saw most of his rounds hit the zigzagging hovercraft's skirt and lower hull. It didn't even slow her down. With a flash, they were past her and climbing back up for a second run. As they flashed past the pilothouse, Mugabe saw the twinkle of assault rifle fire from the mercenaries on deck. Those boys weren't about to hang it up yet.

As soon as they were in the clear, Mugabe turned and looked over his shoulder to see that One Three's attack had fared no better than theirs had. If anything, the boat was going even faster.

Rolling out of his climb, Wolff stomped down on his rudder pedal, snapping the tail of the Griffin around. "Stop that son of a bitch this time!" he snapped.

"Fly this fucker in a straight line then," the gunner snapped back. "I can't get a good sight picture."

When Wolff came back down, he held a steady line of flight, ignoring the streams of tracers rising to meet them. Mugabe was leaning into his turret controls and as soon as the Griffin was lined up, he centered his gunsight crosshairs on the hovercraft's lift fans and pulled all the way back on his gun triggers.

The Chain Gun roared at its maximum rate of fire. Nine hundred and fifty rounds of 25mm per minute poured into the lift fans of the wildly zigzagging boat. The hail of high explosive fire shredded the fans and chunks of the blades spun off like shrapnel, destroying the housings. With all the lift gone, the hull of the hovercraft settled down into the water.

Mugabe switched his aim to the turbines that drove the craft. Even with the lift fans gone, she could still make way with her hull in the water. Another burst destroyed the turbines and the boat slowed to a stop.

Now it was time to talk to them again.

"You on the hovercraft," Wolff called down through his loud speakers, "Put your weapons down and come up on deck with your hands over your heads."

On the boat, De Lancy raised himself from behind the railing where he had taken cover when the Griffin made its attack. A couple of men were down, but the heavy machine gun on top of the pilothouse was still intact. "Get that chopper!" he yelled up to the men behind the gun as he dropped back down behind cover.

Mugabe caught the movement of the gun crew right as they opened fire. What looked like glowing orange balls rose from the pilothouse and rushed up toward them, twelve point seven mm heavy machine gun rounds. Wolff kicked down on the rudder pedal and slammed the cyclic over against the side stop. The Griffin suddenly dropped off to one side.

"Get them!" Wolff shouted through the radio to his wing man.

Coming in low from the other side, the gunner in One Two opened up with everything he had, 25mm and 40mm all at once. The pilothouse erupted like a bomb had been dropped on it. Men, weapons and chunks of the structure flew up into the air and splashed into the water. An instant later, a secondary explosion rocked the hovercraft sending a ball of flame into the sky.

In the left seat of the speeding Dragon One Four, Sandra Revell peered through her optical gunsight. "We're at absolute max range," she told Gunner. "But I think I can get him."

"Give it a try," he answered, his eyes locked on the gauges of his over-revving turbines.

Sandra's finger slowly closed on the right trigger for the Chain Gun. Laying all the way back, she unleashed the full, awesome power of nine hundred and fifty 25mm rounds a minute, a storm of fire that nothing short of a main battle tank could live through.

Sandra's trigger finger barely caressed the firing controls, sending a six round burst after the fleeing Griffin. The tracers showed that her aim was off to the left. She corrected her aim and fired again.

This time, one of the tracer flares disappeared into the Griffin's tail section. She was on target, but her target was no longer there for a third burst.

Cuervo had racked his machine over in a banking climb to get out of the line of fire. Gunner maneuvered to bring his ship into a good firing position, but again Cuervo dodged out of the way. The Mexican pilot's maneuvering, however, had slowed his headlong flight and now Gunner was closing with him at a blinding speed.

Gunner reached out and flicked the governor switch off over-rev. He hated to admit it, but the renegade Mexican could really fly that thing. It was obvious that this was going to turn into an aerial dog fight. And if it was going to be a dog fight, he wanted maximum maneuverability, not maximum speed. He pulled pitch to the main rotor blades, taking a bigger bite of the cool Gulf air.

It was time to dance.

Chapter 28

High Over the Gulf

Wolff and the other pilot circled their Griffins low over the burning wreckage of the sinking hovercraft. They could see the figures of men in the water, some in camouflaged uniforms and some in civilian clothes, clinging to pieces of floating debris.

Wolff was just about to report the sinking of the hovercraft to Dragon Control when he saw the RPM gauge for the portside turbine start fluctuating. The exhaust gas gauge for the same turbine started creeping up and the oil pressure dropped. The turbine had ingested something, probably a missile fragment or a bullet and it was eating itself up.

"One Two," he radioed as he banked away on a heading back for the Megaplatform. "This is Lead, I've got turbine surge and have to break away to find a place to set down ASAP. Keep a close eye on these guys until the Coasties can get here to pick 'em up."

"This is One Two, copy. I've got 'em. Good luck."

Wolff throttled back on both turbines and set the pitch of his main rotor for maximum efficiency. If they were lucky, the damaged turbine would last long enough to get them back.

"You bring your swim suit?" he asked Mugabe.

Several miles away from the sinking hovercraft, two sharklike Griffins danced a deadly ballet in the sky. Gunner had been able to coax a few extra miles an hour out of his ship and had caught up with Cuervo. But once they had started dueling in the sky, the Mexican pilot proved that he had a natural ability for flying.

But again, not as good as Jennings' years of experience. Every time Cuervo tried to break away and run for it, he found his way blocked by the sleek shape of Gunner's Dragon One Four, her gun turret following his every move. The Mexican was a good pilot, but he wasn't as familiar with the Griffin as Jennings was. There was just no way that he was going to escape unless he tried to shoot his way out.

Since Sandra's first warning shots, neither side had brought their weapons into play again. Gunner and Legs were still trying to recover the stolen Griffin intact and Cuervo was reluctant to fire on people who he considered to be his friends. But time and precious fuel was running out for the renegade Mexican officer. If he was going to make it back safely, he had to make his move soon.

Another five minutes of this and he wouldn't have enough fuel to get to safety in Mexican territory where the TPF couldn't follow him.

Reluctantly, Cuervo reached out and switched on the weapons control pilot override. Now he could control the turret and fire the guns from the right seat using the HUD sight displayed on the inside of his helmet visor. He also reached over and turned the radio over to the ship to ship frequency.

Suddenly, his helmet earphones were filled with Gunner's voice. ". . . and bring it around on a heading back to the platforms. Cuervo, do you copy? . . . Answer me damnit! . . . Dragon One Three, this is One Four. You cannot escape. Bring your ship . . .''

Cuervo keyed his throat mike. "I hear you Gunner," he said calmly.

" 'Bout fucking time," Gunner snapped back. "Just what in the hell do you think you are doing? Lock your weapons turret and turn back for the platforms."

"I'm sorry, Gunner," Cuervo radioed. "But I cannot do that."

"If you don't," Gunner's voice was hard. "I'm going to blast your ass out of the sky."

Cuervo didn't answer, he was too busy looking for an opening, a shot that would disable Gunner's ship and let him get away. Both choppers had slowed down for maximum maneuverability and the way they were dancing all over the sky; it was hard for him to get a clear shot.

Suddenly, One Four flashed past in front of his ship giving him the shot he wanted. He reflexively pulled back on the Chain Gun trigger and felt the air frame shake as the big gun hammered. He saw his tracers go wide and gently nudged down on the rudder pedal to correct his aim.

Gunner saw the flash of Cuervo's cannon from the corner of his eye and threw his ship into evasive maneuvers. Suddenly, his ship wasn't where it had been an instant before.

Cuervo followed Gunner through his evasive maneuvers and got in a couple more shots at them, but somehow, the rounds always went wide. The thought flashed through Sandra's mind that he was not really trying to hit them, but she killed that idea. This was an aerial dog fight and there could only be one winner in this contest. There were no prizes for second place in aerial combat.

Finally, Gunner broke away and tried to get into a firing position behind the other chopper. Now, he learned how well Cuervo could fly. As hard as he tried, he could not get on the Mexican's tail. Sandra tried to follow the wildly gyrating Griffin through the sky, but wasn't able to find a shot, any shot.

179

"Taclink!" she suddenly shouted. "Activate the Taclink!"

By activating the system, anything that Cuervo did with his ship would show up on Gunner's tactical monitor before the Griffin reacted.

Gunner reached out and activated the Taclink and switched it over to receive input from One Three. Suddenly, his tactical monitor came alive with the data sent from Cuervo's onboard computer. Now he had him!

The Mexican pilot feinted to the right, but the Taclink told Gunner that he was holding left pedal and was looking to his left, waiting to make his move. Gunner also feinted to the right, but snapped back to the left just as Cuervo made his move. Gunner's ship slid in right behind One Three's tail and Sandra gave him a short burst.

Cuervo still had his ECM module engaged and with only her optical sights to shoot with, Sandra saw her tracers miss the wildly gyrating Griffin. "Closer!" she shouted. "Get in closer! I can't follow him!"

Gunner twisted his throttle and pulled in closer behind Cuervo. The Mexican was throwing his machine all over the sky, but he could not shake Gunner off his ass. Like a pit bull, Gunner was not about to let him go.

Sandra fired another short burst and watched the tracers flash within a foot of the Griffin. She corrected her aim and fired again, a long burst this time.

One Three staggered under the hits. The armor-piercing 25mm rounds tore their way through the armor-plating and smashed into the portside turbine, shattering the spinning compressor blades. The turbine nacelles were armor-plated, but the plating was not thick enough to withstand the heavy caliber, high explosive Chain Gun rounds.

The stolen Griffin shuddered as the turbine seized. The ruined engine automatically declutched, but not before the broken compressor blades cut through the oil and hydraulic lines. The spurting oil was ignited by the red hot burner cans. Flames spouted from the jagged rents in the armored skin and whipped back into the slip stream.

With one turbine out and the hydraulics damaged, the ship rolled over onto her side and Cuervo fought to regain control. For a few precious seconds, he was almost stationary in the sky as Gunner bored in even closer behind him.

Catching another good shot, Sandra fired again, walking her rounds down into the belly of the ship and piercing the fuel tanks. The JP-4 jet fuel whipped back into the slip stream and was ignited by the burning oil. A third burst tore into the masthead and disabled the rotor controls. The rotor blades feathered and Dragon One Three nosed over and dropped out of the sky, all her lift gone.

Trailing fire, the shattered Griffin fell toward the water. Gunner followed the stricken ship down to try to rescue Cuervo if he survived the crash, But right above the wave tops, Dragon One Three exploded in a ball of angry red and black flames.

Sandra turned her head away for a second, but turned back to watch the burning fragments of the chopper impact into the Gulf. Gunner dropped even lower and flew a circle over the crash site, but nothing could be seen except for small bits of debris floating on the water.

Dragon One Three and Arturo Cuervo had vanished beneath the waves.

He made another pass over the wave tops and keyed his throat mike. "Dragon Control, this in One Four," Gunner radioed. "The intruder Griffin has been splashed at coordinates eight-three-seven, two-five-six. There are no sign of survivors. How copy?"

"One Four, this is Control," came Mom's calm voice. "Good copy. We'll pass that information on to the Coast Guard. Return to operational control."

"Good copy," Gunner answered as he slowly banked his ship around. "One Four, clear."

Sandra looked down at the water one last time before sitting back and switching her weapons off. It was a done thing now and there was nothing she could do about it. As with any other police shooting in the line of duty, all she could no now was to live with it. She had killed before and

181

she would kill again. It was something that went with the job.

"Tac Two, Tac Two this is Dragon One Zero, declaring an in-flight emergency," Wolff radioed down to the Tac Team holding the central control platform as he approached the Megaplatform complex. By now, the entire complex was in the hands of Zoomie's men. "Better get that fucking landing pad cleared ASAP."

"Tac Two, copy. We'll get right on it."

"You'd fucking better!" Wolff shouted. "We're coming down whether you're clear down there or not!"

With one eye on the wildly fluctuating portside turbine RPM, Wolff fought the controls as he watched the black uniformed figures of the Tac Team struggle to roll the full oil barrels out of the way. As soon as an adequate space had been made in the middle of the small square of the helipad, Wolff guided his crippled Griffin down to a landing on the central control platform.

Right as he touched down, the exhaust gas temperature gauge shot all the way off the dial and the damaged turbine destroyed itself with a banshee-like shriek. He toggled the switch for the on-board fire extinguisher and hit the fuel cutoff. As the shrieking died, he popped the release to his shoulder harness and exited the aircraft as fast as he could.

Mugabe was hot on his heels.

A safe distance away, the two flyers turned back to see if their wounded bird would go up in flames. All it did, however, was trail a tendril of thin black smoke from the ruined turbine.

"Man, you've got to stop doing that shit," Mugabe said quietly, shaking his head.

"What do you mean, Mojo?" Wolff grinned as he pulled his helmet off and ran his fingers through his hair. "I got us down safely didn't I?"

"Shee-it!"

Since their Griffin was in no danger of exploding or catching fire, Wolff returned to the cockpit, switched the radio back on and keyed the mike. "Dragon Control, this is Dragon Lead."

"Control, go."

"This is Lead. Advise Command One that we are now in control of the Megaplatform. Please inform Dragon maintenance that we have one Griffin that's in drastic need of a turbine change."

"Control, copy. Do you require air lift to bring that ship to this station?"

"This is Lead, that's a negative at this time. I think that I can fly it back on the other engine, but Tac One will need an alternate ride home for some of his people. I don't want to risk transporting them in a damaged ship."

"Control, copy. Anything further?"

"Dragon Lead, negative. Clear."

"Now what do we do?" Mugabe asked.

"Let's see if the other turbine is still good," Wolff said. "And, if it is, we'll go home."

"About fucking time," Mugabe muttered. "I think I need a shot of tequila."

"I thought you didn't drink that stuff?"

"There's a first time for everything."

Chapter 29

Bolen Air Base

As soon as Wolff and Mugabe arrived back at Bolen Air Base, Buzz called a meeting of the chopper cops to give them the final update on the results of the mission.

Buzz was in high spirits when he walked into the briefing room. "Okay, people," he said. "Here's the story. Except for a few miscellaneous bullet holes, the Megaplatform is intact and is back in the hands of the oil company people. They say that they will have it back into production early next week. Congratulations are in order for your not having trashed it too badly in the course of the operation. Also, the Coast Guard and the EPA have the oil spill under control and will have it mopped up before it can do too much damage to the fishing grounds. Again, congratulations, you saved the shrimp population and Cajun cuisine for future generations.''

He flipped through the report in his hands. "Now to the accounting. We took eighteen mercenaries into custody, including a self-styled Captain Geoffry De Lancy, their commander. He is cooperating fully with the investigation and arrest warrants have been served against certain members of the board of directors of United Petroleum, Limited in Great Britain.''

"Casualties among the mercenaries were fairly heavy,'' Buzz continued reading. "Eight were killed, another twelve wounded and three of them are still missing and presumed dead. The Coast Guard also fished the body of the late Travis Cunningham III of Cunningham Oil out of the Gulf.''

He paused for a moment. "So far, however, no sign has been found of the wreckage of Dragon One Three or of Lieutenant Cuervo's body. Nor has the Arab mercenary known as Falcon been found.''

"You will be pleased to learn that our own casualties were light considering the scope of this operation. Zoomie will be back with us in no time at all and only one of his six men wounded is in serious condition. All told, it was a job very well done.''

"Washington is putting through a TPF unit citation for this affair and . . .'' He looked directly at Sandra. "Several officers have been cited for acts of individual heroism as well.''

"As soon as we can get packed up, we'll be going back to Denver. And for those of you with families, we should arrive well before Thanksgiving. Those of you, however, who are planning to celebrate the holiday in our own Tac Force mess hall, might want to consider staying down here for another week or so."

Everyone broke out laughing.

"That's it for now, get your gear ready and standby for movement orders."

Buzz searched out Wolff in the crowd. "Wolfman, I'd like to see you for a moment."

As the room emptied, Wolff made his way to the front of the room. "Yes sir?"

"Come on into the office."

Wolff walked in and Buzz closed the door behind him. "I've got something here that I think you might want to take a look at," Buzz said picking a folder up off his desk. "I just got this faxed in from the Mexican authorities." He handed the folder to the pilot.

Wolff opened the folder and saw that it was the report of an investigation on Lieutenant Arturo Cuervo. He quickly read through it and handed it back to his commander.

"There had to have been something else he could have done about this," he said shaking his head. "He didn't need to have gone along with Cunningham's scheme."

"I know," Buzz said. "But there's no way that we can know what he was thinking at the time. It's hard to lose land that's been in your family for generations."

"Can I let my people know about this?" Wolff asked.

"Maybe you should," Buzz said. "I'm sure there are some of them who would feel better for knowing the pressures he was under."

Buzz hadn't mentioned any specific names, but Wolff knew exactly who he was referring to. "I'll take care of it," he said.

As soon as Buzz was finished with him, Wolff went looking for Legs. He wanted to talk to her about what he had read about Cuervo and to reassure her that she had done

185

the right thing by shooting him down. As the Dragon Flight leader, he would have done the same for any of his gunners. But with her, of course, there was more to it than just good leadership.

The first place he looked for her was on the flight line where the air crews were checking over their choppers for the long flight home. No one there, though, had seen her and he headed for the maintenance office.

"Yo! Red!" he called through the open door. "You seen Legs?"

"Nope," the maintenance chief shook his head. "but I need to talk to you about . . ."

"Save it," Wolff said curtly as he spun around and walked off.

"Hey, wait a minute," Red shouted. "I need . . ."

Wolff was already out of earshot and headed for the club only to find it empty. He then checked in the officers' quarters, but she wasn't there either. He finally went out to the main gate and asked the guard on duty if he had seen a tall blond female chopper cop leave the base in the last half hour or so.

"I saw her head out to the road and catch a ride with someone," the gate guard said.

"Oh shit!" Wolff said. "Did you see which way she was heading? And what kind of car did she get into?"

"They went south," the airman pointed, toward the coast. "In some rancher's beat up old blue pickup."

The pilot took off running back to the hanger. "Mojo!" he yelled when he saw his gunner. "Quick! I need the key to your bike!"

"What's up?"

"I got to go after Legs."

Mugabe flipped him the key for the Kawasaki. "Watch it now," he warned.

Wolff ignored him as he put the magnetically coded key into the ignition and fired up the powerful bike. He hit first gear, popped the clutch and left a patch of rubber on the tarmac as he accelerated for the main gate. He turned south onto the Texas state highway and opened up the throttle.

Where in the hell did she think she was going?

He spent the next hour hitting every place he could think of where she might have gone, every public beach and every park along the road. Several times, he stopped and talked to people, but no one had seen her. Then he thought of Big Jim's Ribs where he and Mojo had seen her that night with the Mexican pilot. Spinning the big bike around, he took off as if he had been shot.

A quick check of the restaurant turned up nothing, but he left the bike in the parking lot and headed down to the beach. Once past the scrub brush at the storm line, he spotted a solitary figure standing at the water's edge and headed for it at a run hoping that it was Sandra. As he got closer, he saw that it was.

"Sandra," he called out as he approached her.

She slowly turned to face him and he saw that her face was calm. "Rick, what are you doing here?" She sounded surprised. "How did you find me?"

"Oh," he said, embarrassed now that she seemed to be okay. "When I found out that you had taken off, I wanted to make sure that you were okay, so I just cruised around asking myself where I would have gone if I wanted to be alone."

"I'm okay," she said, stiffly. "You didn't have to check up on me."

"Well," he answered, digging the toe of his flying boot into the silver sand. "I just wanted to see if there was anything I could do. I mean, I know it's tough sometimes to have to drop the hammer on someone. And we've worked together for so long that I just thought . . ."

Wolff's voice tapered off. He realized that nothing he was saying really made much sense. And he knew that he was lying. He had come to find her because he loved her and he hoped that she would come to him for comfort if she needed a shoulder to cry on.

"Ah, shit," he tried to start again, but stopped, not

wanting to expose too much of his feelings until he knew what she was thinking about Cuervo. "I just wanted to help if I could."

"Thanks for caring, but I'm fine." She sounded very sure of that. "I had a job to do and I did it."

"I know," Wolff said. "But I thought that maybe this time it was going to be different."

"Why?" Sandra's voice was hard. "Just because I went to bed with him one time?"

Now that it was out in the open, Wolff could meet her eyes squarely. "Yes," he said. "I thought that might make it different."

"It might have," she snapped. "If I were some fluffy headed, bimbo civilian. Remember, Rick, I'm as good a cop as any man on the force."

"Damnit," he hated being on the defensive with her. "I know that. Man or woman, it's got to hurt. I'm just trying to . . ."

"I know it, Rick, I know. Thanks."

"Why did he do it?" she asked, suddenly. "It didn't have to end this way. When he came to help Gunner and me, I thought that he'd had a change of heart. He saved our lives back there."

"Well," Wolff said, glad to be off the hot seat. "We've found out that he was desperately in need of money, a lot of money. His family holdings were in danger of being confiscated by the Mexican government for back taxes they owed. Apparently, the recent drought had just about wiped his family out and he . . ."

"No," she said softly, shaking her head. "That's not what I mean. Why did he do this to us, to all of us, not just me? Did he come on to me just so he could get the information he needed to betray us to the terrorists?"

Wolff shook his head. "I don't think we'll ever know that," he said.

She was quiet for a long moment.

"How about coming back now," Wolff finally said. "Buzz wants us to start packing up to go home."

Sandra looked out over the Gulf of Mexico one last time. "Okay," she said, softly. "I guess its time."

She turned back to the pilot, reaching out to touch his arm. "Thanks for finding me, Rick. It helps to talk to a friend."

"Glad to help," Wolff replied, stuffing his hands in his pockets.

Neither one of them said a word as they walked back up to the parking lot where he had left Mugabe's bike. He climbed on it and she slid in behind him straddling the jump seat. As soon as he fired the big Kawasaki up and started for the road, she slipped her arms around his waist to hold on.

A helicopter flashed overhead and both of them automatically looked up. But it was not one of the Dragon Flight Griffins. Their choppers were waiting for them back on the flight line.

MYSTIC REBEL by Ryder Syvertsen

WARBOTS by G. Harry Stine

#5 OPERATION HIGH DRAGON (17-159, $3.95)

Civilization is under attack! A "virus program" has been injected into America's polar-orbit military satellites by an unknown enemy. The only motive can be the preparation for attack against the free world. The source of "infection" is traced to a barren, storm-swept rock-pile in the southern Indian Ocean. Now, it is up to the forces of freedom to search out and destroy the enemy. With the aid of their robot infantry—the Warbots—the Washington Greys mount Operation High Dragon in a climactic battle for the future of the free world.

#6 THE LOST BATTALION (17-205, $3.95)

Major Curt Carson has his orders to lead his Warbot-equipped Washington Greys in a search-and-destroy mission in the mountain jungles of Borneo. The enemy: a strongly entrenched army of Shiite Muslim guerrillas who have captured the Second Tactical Battalion, threatening them with slaughter. As allies, the Washington Greys have enlisted the Grey Lotus Battalion, a mixed-breed horde of Japanese jungle fighters. Together with their newfound allies, the small band must face swarming hordes of fanatical Shiite guerrillas in a battle that will decide the fate of Southeast Asia and the security of the free world.

#7 OPERATION IRON FIST (17-253, $3.95)

Russia's centuries-old ambition to conquer lands along its southern border erupts in a savage show of force that pits a horde of Soviet-backed Turkish guerrillas against the freedom-loving Kurds in their homeland high in the Caucasus Mountains. At stake: the rich oil fields of the Middle East. Facing certain annihilation, the valiant Kurds turn to the robot infantry of Major Curt Carson's "Ghost Forces" for help. But the brutal Turks far outnumber Carson's desperately embattled Washington Greys, and on the blood-stained slopes of historic Mount Ararat, the high-tech warriors of tomorrow must face their most awesome challenge yet!

Available wherever paperbacks are sold, or order direct from the Publisher. Send cover price plus 50¢ per copy for mailing and handling to Pinnacle Books, Dept.17-400, 475 Park Avenue South, New York, N.Y. 10016. Residents of New York, New Jersey and Pennsylvania must include sales tax. DO NOT SEND CASH.